TAP AND DIE

LANCELOT SCHAUBERT

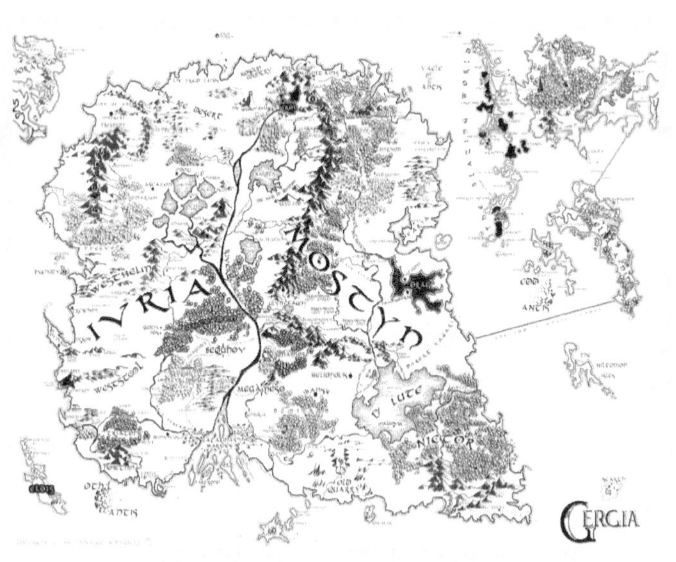

IVRIA
NOSTYN
SEAHOV
MEGA DEGO
LUTE
NICCOR
OTHI
ELOIS
CERGIA

I

HONORIFICS

The driver looked cockeyed at Black Jack Dawes's half-frozen hands that held the other reins. The driver took kings and nobles all over the Ivrian side of the world, not crusty old tradesmen in khaki dusters, range hats, knee-high boots slathered in mud, and that black cloak with those unfixed stars on it. And no sword? But it was Black Jack's knuckles that drew the driver's focus. They were as frozen as two hands could get: white on a purple field.

"Renaud's," Jack explained. "No circulation in extremities. Plus I hate going—"

The team of horses sped over the downy green hillock and the many-wheeled carriage got air. Jack's knuckles went whiter. His feet slammed into the foothold and his back braced even deeper into the red velvet seat cushions. As wheels hit earth, the old range man grunted, "—fast."

"Oh, sorry, Your Excellence, I—"

"No ambassador. Nor emissary."

"Your wife is."

"So bill her, cut the titles."

The driver nodded.

"Honorifics," Jack said and spat. "Every horse breeder, every smith's apprentice, every cloth merchant from here to Tetra has some sort of gold salesman-of-the-month plaque, some jade crystal award for the same shit they do every day. Here's a cheap piece of metal that *looks* a little like the metal we named this plaque after in order to celebrate the thing you're already doing just to survive." He threw up a little in his mouth in a not-subtle way. "Fool's gold is still for fools even if you make a trophy out—"

The carriage caught air again, and Jack almost puked.

"I'll slow down a bit," said the driver.

"I'm not... I'm not queasy." Jack gagged again, audibly. "I'll be fine I just... *hnngh*... I just don't like feeling like I'm flying through the air, that's all."

"You fly often?" The driver chuckled.

"The boss has me do it far more often than I like."

"Here, for your hands." The driver took the reins in one hand and passed over a pair of gloves.

"I have gloves."

"These are entangled with lava. They're constantly warm, plus they'll help with the nerves."

Jack Dawes raised an eyebrow.

"Trust me. Once you get there—you're changing, right?"

Black Jack looked down at his outer wear, confused.

The driver chuckled. "*I* wouldn't go to an inaugural ball looking like that."

"I hate these things."

"Okay, so when you're all stripped down between outfits, put these gloves on and put them on the mirror."

"Why do I have to be naked?"

"Shhhh, trust the process."

Black Jack raised his eyebrow.

"Allow the mirror to fog and let the room steam up and you'll feel completely warm. That's why naked."

"Wouldn't I be warmer with clothes too?"

"No. Plus you're naked so you realize it more, just trust the process! Only downside to these things is they attract lava and magma, but it's not like you're going to the surface of some star."

Black Jack had done that before. He didn't recommend it. "Know what I hate about inaugural balls?"

The driver waited, sipping his cocoa out of his copper longcup, which had long gone cold.

"There's always some inauguration or convocation or launch of some new ship that needs christening for some maiden voyage. People start shit far more often than they finish shit. For once, I want a *terminal* ball. Celebrate the death of something. Or its culmination at least."

The driver looked again at the black cloak, and it reminded him of the angel of death. Poking out of the vest pocket was a crowfoot attached to a long bone, sharpened to a point.

"The Crowfoot Mile?" he asked.

Jack grimaced. He hated that people only remembered that part of it.

"You're a Storyweaver?"

"That's what the cloak is for."

The driver truly saw it for the first time, and his eyes widened. Then he focused on the road ahead. "Don't you think the new military allegiance between the Common Realms puts guys like you out of work?"

"I wish it had."

2

THE HOLLOW NEEDLE

The Hollow Needle did not rise above the horizon, but sank into the great peak of Weststool, steam and smoke heralding it in a great circular halo. One of five new taps in Gergia, the opposite of towers, it drilled down into a too-wide hole. Seven carriage bridges—long stone pathways lit by gas lamps—led from the ridge of the hole to a midair platform, and that platform formed the base of a great spire that sank down into the hot airy heart of an active volcano, the bubbling lava a mere sixty feet deeper than the tap's lowest basement, the observation deck. Gravity had been inverted around the outside of the tap building so that the heat close to the building's surface would first vent *down* toward the lava while heavier things went *up* toward the surface. But once outside that ring of gravity inversion, the steam would vent *up* once more, farther away from the tap. The result was a ring of steam and smoke around the outer rim, but a sort of a dead-air protective circle the closer you got to the tap's walls and entrance.

Inside the tap's combined fortieth, forty-first, and forty-second floors, the various ambassadors from around Ivria and most of Mostyn (and isles and antics) had gathered. They banqueted a new year of new staff and new policy initiatives, but really it was an excuse for well-connected wealthy people to get together and celebrate whatever culinary and aesthetic discovery one of their member realms had drummed up. (That, and negotiate terms of various deals, both aboveboard and under the table and backhanded.)

This year, the new delicacy was a sort of bowl made of a star-shaped grain called *sfensü* (named after the local word *sfen* for "vintage" and the ablative case: something *extracted away from* the vintage). Sfensü grew on mile-long vines with leaves so massive you could build a house on them, vines that now draped down into the Old Quarry through the remnants of the Sicilian that had been mined out of the planet's heart. In addition to the sfensü base, the delicacy used wild Imperial Crescent skyhog for the protein, and the entire affair was garnished with shaved pomace from some off-world persimmon and then topped with a Blazing World molasses. Sort of a culinary incarnation of the principle of Common Realms.

That was why most of them had come.

That, and the backdoor deals.

Frey had brought her daughter, Dövë (named after the Aruöfian word for ocean as well as the earthbound term for a bird of peace, a compromise she'd made with Jack). Dövë attended her mother to the main table, but Frey soon retreated to her office overlooking the landing on the forty-third floor, which in turn overlooked the banquet. From here she could see the folks in great flamboyant headgear and the most spartan skin-colored suits you could imagine moving around the cosmopolitan panoply of ambassadors.

The main color present was a dark grey, but that only tended to offset the other colors all the more vibrantly, city sidewalk and holiday style.

A man rose from the table from where Frey had left Dövë and went up to Frey's office. "Why don't you come dance with me?" he asked Frey.

"Sfòne." She blushed every time she was forced to say his name, but she hid it better each time. She refused to translate it for her colleagues. "No thank you."

"Ask again later," he said. "Got it." He returned to the table.

Dövë watched him descend one of the many open and white marble spiral staircases that connected some of the floors. She watched him descend the whole way.

When he returned to his seat, she said, "My dad's coming."

"Oh?" Sfòne said.

3
DÖVË

Dövë had been precocious from a very, very young age. By her eleventh month, she was speaking full sentences. By the fifteenth, two languages. By her second year, she could read by herself. By herself, alone in a room, two languages. An incredible mind for most children, though others might have beaten her.

By the age of four, she had read all of the children's books in her local library, the regional library, and the capital library—and she did it systematically so as not to overlook any cultures, any voices, any intellectual "foods" she didn't like. After that, she decided that the best of the adult world would be her oyster. So she moved on to the classics.

Her parents, however, ignored her. Both Jack and Frey. They seemed so preoccupied with themselves and their debate about... well, to Dövë it seemed like some complicated form of flirting. So she decided to pull pranks in order to get their attention. Once she glued her father's belt to his pant loops and buckle so that he couldn't pull them off. Jack struggled and struggled against it until he wet his pants. She giggled in secret over that. Her dad's urine weaving skills could dry his pants quickly, but she had been delighted as a young girl to see him struggle and rage.

For her mom, Dövë hid a cockatiel in the oven, and the bird talked to her mother and drove her nuts in the kitchen. Days of that, days of laughing over that. Quite hilarious—until Frey lit the oven and murdered the poor bird.

That was what Dövë had come to this ball with: a slew of pranks.

She didn't hate her dad. She adored her dad. And seeing him descend the stairs made her love him even more, want to see him even more.

Her dad was coming.

Her dad was here.

4

GYROCOMPASS

"What's that?" the carriage driver asked, pointing to the black stone gyroscope in Black Jack Dawes's hand. The wheels moved, wheels within wheels.

"Gyrocompass."

"Like on a ship?"

Jack Dawes raised an eyebrow. "How do you know about those?"

"My off-world grandfather works on ships."

"Something like that, only not on a world. It's attuned to the rotation and orbits of all planets, all times, all timelines to orient true to The Clockwork."

"The what?"

"It'll steer you where you need to be, when you need to be, what you need to be and whom and why and how and how much. If you let it. But it can't choose for you, let alone choose well. It's a pipeline to the archive."

The man said, "Archive of law reviews? Dissected insects?" He whipped the reins.

"Everything," Jack said. "Or at least most compasses

connect to the archive. This one's more of a local walkie-talkie."

"A what?"

"You know how when you're standing under one arch of the great dome in the Megameso capital building and your friend's standing at the other, you can hear each other whispering as if you're next to each other even if the place is full of busy, noisy folks?"

"Never been."

"Like that, but no building and no limit on the distance. This one won't connect to the archive."

"Why carry it?"

"So I can give it to drivers I like without worrying if they'll snoop around for dangerous info. Communication channels for events like these come in handy. I'm sure there's another onyx compass just like this inside."

5

BRACER

Frey didn't think Jack would show. Jack hadn't shown for nine months now: she could have been pregnant and had a baby in this time. He was always helping everyone else but her and Dövë. Or it felt that way.

She saw the painting of the three of them surrounded by grandparents and cousins, and flanked by many, many in black world cloaks. Starlings. She took it off the wall and set it behind the bookshelf. It left an undusted, ungreased ghost spot on the wall. On her desk sat a stack of love letters he'd written her while on the road. She took that and tossed it into the top drawer.

Perhaps.

And... this was only a perhaps if Jack didn't show yet again.

Perhaps...

No. She couldn't dance with a man like Sfòne.

But anyway, having the painting down and having the letters in a drawer felt like a nice little jab at her absent husband. For good measure, she took the wedding ring off her right thumb and put it on top of the love letters.

Then she eyed the copper bracer on the desk. The one Sfòne had left her.

6

EMERGENCY HAND CANNONS

The driver smiled at him. "Divorced?"

Black Jack scoffed, grinning at the driver's wit.

"Got sick of me helping everyone else but her and Dövë."

"Whom?"

"My daughter. *Our* daughter. She switched to embassy work down here to help herself."

"Her little quirk being a self-sufficient ambassador wasn't worth your time to help? You didn't want to move and help her?"

Jack said nothing.

"Cause it wasn't part of the story you're helping to weave. You wanted to help her in your own way, not help her with the part she wanted the help on."

"Yeah," Black Jack said. And scoffed again and smirked. He was impressed.

"Now that it demands your help — now that you got to come down here — you have to stop and fix what she prefers." They pulled up to the carriage line, with the great steam and smoke rising in a ring around the base of the tap.

Black Jack pointed to a sign: *WATCH FOR FALLING ROCKS.* "What rocks?" he said. "Mountain's clear."

"They vent the lava flow beneath by reverse gravity around the walls of the tap."

"Why?"

"Protects the surface of the building."

A great stone shot up into the air on the far end of the tap, arcing through the air until gravity reasserted itself, and then it fell straight for the platform. It crashed down to the side.

"What in the name of the Byline..." Jack said. "Why don't they protect these people?"

"If security needs to move a rock midair, they will."

"What if they're gone?"

"Then you have much bigger problems than falling rocks. It's just a light show that *feels* dangerous. Our horses are fine."

Carriages poured out of the various spokes of the platform's wheel, but this last bridge was reserved for those now arriving. Black Jack hopped down, turned back to the driver, and nodded at the compass. "Didn't get your name?"

"Krif Chtāysū Hochtālyi."

"Klūhman?" Jack asked. "What's Ktæsû mean? To disrupt..."

"Disrupt a result. Theorize an outcome. Disturb an ending. Normally just Retriever."

"Huh. I guess a getaway driver does disrupt a result. And if he's your get-*to* driver, he theorizes an outcome. Can I call you Fetch?"

"All my Ivrian friends do."

"Don't feel like a dog?"

"Everyone is a dog in my culture. Krif is an honorific that means *dog.* Foreigners like you are stray mutts." He nodded to the muddy outfit. "But there's only one white wolf."

Black Jack thought. "Hang on to that compass."

"If it goes badly, dome-whisper and we can ride. I'll be reading." He held up a book. "Bizarre novel about creatures called *cowboys*. They wield small emergency hand cannons, but they use them *all the time*. Wasteful, that quantity of brimstone. Perhaps it's meant for only the very, very rich? Yet I enjoy the novel so."

The rich. Westerns. Black Jack shook his head and headed down the path.

His foot scuffed something, and he almost tripped headlong, but caught himself. Turning, he looked to see what it was. A jagged, yellow stone had barred his way. He bent down and picked it up, his heart stirring. It looked like a block of sulfur, and had it been, it would have been a very clever find indeed. But as fool's gold fools prospectors, so this yellow stone had fooled an old brimstone weaver like him. He put it in his hat, tucked into the little compartment he kept at the top. For luck.

7

SOARING DOWN

The main attendant scrolled through. And scrolled through. "No Dawes other than a young girl."

Jack's daughter. And his wife?

"Try Frey Sfansòrsi?." The last sound came out as if someone had grabbed his throat and choked him halfway through. That was how Frey had taught him: choking off his airway with her nails while grinning.

"Miss Sfansòrsi? is right at the top."

"Missus," he said.

"Take the nib out of the well and write down the floor you need," said the attendant. "In this case, forty-first. It summons a carved limestone pod that will fall up toward us. Write the floor again inside to confirm, and the reverse gravity will release and you will fly down to your floor. Have you never seen a descender such as this?"

"They call them elevators where I spend most of my time. They work the opposite in every way."

"How odd, Good Sir Dawes. Enjoy."

Sir. Pfft.

Jack wrote down a calligraphic 41, and two stone doors

opened without a hint of a sound, revealing a hand-carved box large enough to stand in. He stepped inside, started to write *41*, and then wrote *42* instead. Instantly he felt the sensation of dropping. Even going as slow as the thing went, he hated that feeling. That feeling of...

Soaring down...

Soaring down...

...into the belly of the planet Gergia.

"Floor forty-two. Enjoy your visit."

He exited into much color and noise. The curved and floating shapes of people filled the landings above and below in silks and linens and wools and armor made of papier-mâché and chains topped with asymmetrical hats and other metal headgear. None would ride well on a horse, disguise well in the wild, or protect well from lightning or spear. No weaponry other than the collective armed force from the best troops of each nation of the Common Realms: trained as one, polyglots all, and defenders all of their homeland of all lands. Or all *participating* lands.

Something in Jack's poorer upbringing made him think of how he was dressed. He didn't like thinking of his Pit-damned outfit.

He scanned the crowd—and locked eyes with his little girl.

Dövë, he mouthed.

"*Dad!*" she screamed over her table's guests.

The guests looked at her and looked at where she was looking and saw Jack, looking down not on them, but his girl. But his eyes had moved, and when they turned to follow his gaze, Dövë had moved as well, sprinting up the closest ramp from the forty-first landing to the forty-second.

Jack didn't sprint, but he did hustle his long bow-legged strides.

They collided on the second step. She always hugged him tighter than anything. He felt the swelling of twenty-one bows on twenty-one heartstrings, a swell that vibrated his tear ducts. A great cathedral opened in him, one he could not quite shut the door upon, one that spoke of his bit role in this passion play.

8

TO THRIVE

At five and a half, Dövë had gone off to school in The Tap at the request of her mother. Both the daycare and babysitters like Sfòne had watched over Dövë, and Sfòne in particular, astonished by Dövë's prowess in all things—though he ascribed it only to the mother and not to the father— had taken an interest in getting the girl tutors, and in finding her a mentor for her mind and powers.

Frey wanted nothing to do with this. She didn't want the tutors. She didn't want the mentor.

Dövë had thought this was because Frey didn't want her to thrive, to succeed. She told her as much.

Sfòne, half wringing his hands, had fed this fire in hopes of ingratiating himself with the girl.

Frey didn't notice. But in the end, she didn't care about the ends so much as the means. She didn't know if she wanted Sfòne getting that close to her daughter, both on account of Jack—her still-husband in her mind—and on account of Dövë's safety. Who knew what kind of man Sfòne was, deep down?

Sfòne wanted to find the right mentor. He told Dövë as much.

Dövë thought she had to thrive. She had to. She felt as if she'd burst otherwise.

That was all before Dövë ran up to hug her father, Jack Dawes.

9

SEX RITUALS

"**J**ack?" a woman said behind him.

He turned, his girl in hand, and barrel-carried her, flailing and giggling, up the two steps to meet his wife.

"Frey," he said. "You clean up good, young lady."

She smiled curtly. "The job."

She looked at his boots.

He expected scorn.

What he got was, "I would sooner accompany you on the trails than these others."

"Why don't you?" he asked.

"Because, Jackson Daweson, on the trail it grows difficult to notice when your wife and daughter have need of your help more than some stranded traveler."

He winced.

An elder statesman walked up with skin tinged green.

Frey said, "Jack Dawes, my boss, Krif Hemē Kraswa."

"Good to meet you, you dog," Jack said.

Frey blushed. "*Jack!*"

But Hemē smiled. "You know Klūhman culture better than your wife?"

Frey looked between them both.

"Nah, I just ask different questions," Jack said. "What's the name mean?"

Frey looked between the two of them again, out of her depth.

"Kraswa is a season. Hemē is warm."

"Summer?" Jack asked.

"Yes, but as a name—"

"A Great Fien. Hot weather dog. Big dog," Jack said. "Stately and great for hunting. Good to meet you, Great Fien."

Hemē grinned and looked at the muddy wear of Black Jack Dawes. "That wisdom for a foreigner... yes, I sense that would make you not Krif, but Trulas U. Wolf of the Sun."

Jack felt a mild shock. "But there's only one?"

"One *white* wolf. But to be a dog of Sister Wild is a great honor. To be *born* a dog outside the city, with a pack, and to see other dogs for who they are. This is to be a wolf of honor. And you are hunter of men and hunter of deep ideas and of the lightweaver. I will file the forms to make you Wolf of the Sun. Trulas U."

"Trul... Trul like music?" Frey asked, desperate to get a handhold in the sea of diplomacy she had been thrown into by her husband.

"Trul means music, yes. As for the best..." The music of the ball almost overwhelmed Hemē's words, and he grimaced at it. "The best music is a wolf—U—Trulas U—in the wild on the hunt, patter of paw on the plain in search of sweeter prey. Shall we go somewhere we might hear better?"

They walked the river-shaped walkway on the forty-second floor, the long ramp-shaped walkway that carved a white arc across the back of the ballroom— one step up, five steps forward, one step up. The bank of administrative offices overlooked the pageantry and meetings and tables.

Hēme opened the door to Frey's office, revealing Sfòne. He was seated in her office chair, his open palm on fire, his eyes rolled back in his head.

Frey gasped.

Hēme cleared his throat.

Sfòne snapped to attention and threw the fistful of what remained of the methaqualoin into the galvanized steel trashcan.

Frey and Hēme had already entered the office, but Jack stood in the doorway and kept Dövë at his back to spare her the sight.

Sfòne stood and extended his still-smoking black palm to Jack. "Sfòne. Nice to meet you."

Frey blushed at his name.

Jack never used honorifics. Never. But something boiled in his chest. "Captain Black Jack Dawes, first division of Storyweaver Private Council, tier one Archive, privy counsel to Nerari."

He did not take the proffered hand, but glared at it instead.

Sfòne turned to Frey. "Did you show your husband the bracer I—we, the office—gave you?"

"No," Frey said.

"Show him."

"No."

"You'll love it, Jack. Golden inlay. Made for this tap. An anti-gravity bracer, good as any collar. Keeps you from falling up to your death on the surface if you find yourself outside the wall or stuck in a shaft." He nodded toward the floor and the lift shafts outside the office.

"I'll talk with you later," Hēme said to Sfòne, pointing with his pinky out the door.

Sfòne left, tail tucked.

"Apologies," Hēme said. "Wonderful negotiator and salesman. Terrible at tending himself. I presume you have extra dignitary clothes that will fit your husband?"

Jack pursed his upper lip so as to block his nostrils.

"Of course," Frey said, grinning.

With a nod, her boss departed, closing the door behind him after waving Dövë inside.

"Sfansòrsi??" Jack said.

Frey didn't move.

"You put Sfansòrsi? as your surname on the manifest in the atrium."

Frey said, "Can you stay with me? The kids would love that."

"*Please*, dad?" Dövë begged.

Jack grimaced at his daughter and turned back to Frey. "One second. When did Sfansòrsi? become a thing?"

"It's an Aruöfian office. I needed an Aruöfian name."

"And an Aruöfian boyfriend?"

Frey didn't answer that.

Jack noticed the edge of the old commissioned painting poking out from behind the bookshelf. He looked for, but could not find, the love letters he'd painstakingly composed for her. His lettering wasn't too good, so writing them took forever.

Frey's sleeve fell to her elbow to expose the bracer the addict had given her.

Jack scoffed at it.

"Daddy..." Dövë said, looking between the two.

"Change into something presentable," Frey said.

Black Jack grumbled. "For Dövë. For tonight."

"I must give my policy speech," Frey said. "Dövë, come."

"Can't I stay?" she pleaded.

"Daddy must change. Then join you at table."

"Oh, good."

"On what?" Jack asked.

"Brimstone shortages," Frey said. "And water rights for Forayn."

"They don't dig on off years?"

She smiled. "Not everything comes down to sex rituals, Jack."

He glanced at his daughter.

Who seemed none the wiser.

Jack looked at his wife while pointing at his daughter. "Kay." He watched them pass through the smoked glass door and, in blurry silhouettes, walk down the walkway in front of the big bay window. The shadow of his daughter's hand waved as the rest of her form was pulled ahead.

Jack then turned to the doom his bride had deemed: a closet full of fabulous men's wear in every shape and size and color.

"Save me. Save from this hell," he prayed to the Author in whom he most certainly did not believe.

IO

SEWING KIT

Upstairs—or down, depending—the man at the front desk in the lobby looked up. A group of men dressed in outfits identical to himself and the rest of security were approaching, but he did not recognize a single one of them. For a group so large, this could not be a shift change. Something at the back of his mind stirred.

"Good evening, sirs," he said.

"Good evening, officer. I wonder if you could help me with something."

The desk guard cocked his head.

The man in the blue uniform and double-breasted brass buttons pulled out a long, slender stylet—what had once, it seemed, been a skewer for holding slabs of meat. His lips moved to some unknowable tongue, and a great static yellow thread snaked up from his backpack, attached to the handle of the meat skewer, and *shot forth from the tip as lightning*.

It blew a smoking hole clean through the desk guard's chest.

The storm of new arrivals pulled swords and ran to meet the suddenly onrushing crowd. Bolt after bolt was sent at them by the guards of the Common Realm's tap, and a couple of the newcomers found themselves cut down before they could get off any lightning. But others among them called up full sheets of that yellow stuff in a great warp.

One called up water from a wineskin at his side. A web string attached to the end of a three-hole punch (though most there had no idea what the purpose of the three-hole punch was). He used the hole punch as a needle and wove the weft of water into the warp of the yellowness. Then he poured liquid electricity into the cracks in the floor, and all the lights not run by gas or other fuel began shuddering.

A second man, an oily-haired type they called Oily Oscar, wove oil into lightning and gathered it up into buckets, then painted the innermost walls with the stuff, creating a sort of makeshift electric fencing on the things they didn't want anyone to touch.

Still others met blade for blade. The captain of the Common Realm's guard—who towered seven feet, three hundred pounds of brawn and bastard sword—charged at a newcomer with red hair pouring from his crown like a waterfall of blood. Steel met steel—one, two, three, four, five, six, seven, eight—and on the ninth the redcrown gutted the captain in a flash of red.

The redcrown giggled.

The captain died.

A comrade of the redcrown finished off the captain with a flash of lightning.

The bell from the descenders rang just as the oilweaver finished painting the floor. An entire platoon of reinforcements emerged from all eight doors to defend the tap—a truly massive quantity of Common Realm guards.

They stepped onto the oil-lightning weave...

And lit up like smoking, lightning-struck evergreen trees.

They dropped to the floor. Dead.

"Sewing kit?" the redcrown asked the now-calm brimstone weavers. "I seem to have nicked my nips."

"Propriety, Krif Luwof. This is a house of diplomacy," said a man in black while rifling through the pockets of a smoking corpse, searching for spare change.

II
FETCH

etch, the driver, was deep in his novel. He heard shouts outside his carriage, but why would that concern him? Tons of men were moving around. The stables had closed so that carriages couldn't get out. Someone had blocked off the exits so that none could leave.

That must be awful for those drivers.

But not for Fetch, who went back to reading on the clock.

12

CRESCENT SOLDIERS

The redcrown, Luwof, and his boss, the man in black—both disguised as Crescent soldiers, like the rest of their contingent—had taken control of the lobby, and now they descended to the lower floors. They de-enchanted and re-enchanted the descenders so that they wouldn't bring people to the surface, but would work only between the fortieth floor and the viewing window down near the end tip of the tap, in the belly of the volcano. On the way, they dimmed or extinguished the lights in the windows that could be seen from the seven bridges and the edge of the crater.

13

THAT MUCH BRIMSTONE

Black Jack Dawes put on the lava gloves Fetch had given him. Apart from the gloves—and his hat, the rock still inside—he stood as naked as a jayber crow. Renaud's is a shitty disease if it's bad, especially for contractors and blue-collar men who like to work outside. Keeps all the toes and fingers on the verge of frostbite and necrotic rot even in cool weather, but the belly fiery and ready to go. The gloves... they did kind of make up for it.

He placed them on the mirror as Fetch had told him. The mirror fogged. He looked at the seven outfits laid out across the offensively large vanity, closed the bathroom door, and felt like drowning. And he *had* drowned many times, Overmorrow and otherwise. He looked to the black gyroscopic compass on the edge of the sink and thought to call the driver and thank him for the gloves, the outfits still haunting his periphery.

A crack of thunder, followed by a flash of lightning, deafened him. Thunder *indoors*. Jack didn't have time to put on clothes, but he saw his Crowfoot on the counter and snagged it, hat on, leaving the compass behind.

He touched the knob of the door. It was cold. No fire. He cracked the door, peeking. The room lay empty but for couches, the various hand-carved behemoth desks, the odd trinkets from odd diplomatic missions he'd never quite understood. Frey negotiated with people while Jack smoked with them. Of course, Frey would have said soldiers smoked and diplomats wined and dined, and only one of those got people killed. Jack would have said it was the whining done while wining and dining that got people killed, that those who whine ended up sending younger and better men to fight in their stead. And they would have argued for an hour. Hell, he was already arguing in his head, and she wasn't even there. Love was—

Thunder cracked again.

He moved past the leathern sofas and dimmed the lights so they wouldn't backlight him against the smoked-glass windows. He went to the next door and cracked it ever so slightly, the wind pressure *whooooooing* through the open space. The building had filled up with men who looked like guards—were it not for the large amount of lightning they sent forth to kill others in the same dress. Many people screamed, and the air smelled of sulfur and static charge and barbecue, a rain-canceled grillout without the rain. The only difference he could see on any of the new guards—other than stylets wielded by these folks dead-set on blowing holes through their opponents—were small backpacks from which they drew their brimstone.

That much brimstone...

Fetch might have pointed out it was the operating budget of any one of the countries in the room.

They swarmed both the forty-first landing and the forty-second, and were already sweeping through the rooms. Jack looked for an exit through the little crack, but saw none. Didn't they have some sort of fire escape in these rooms? Some sort of hatch?

Still naked but for the hat and the warming gloves, Jack went right instead of left, away from the bathroom and deeper into the ambassador's offices, hoping for some sign of... something. He called up a warp of air with his Crowfoot. He wasn't a proper windweaver by any stretch, but any high-ratio warp and low-ratio catalyst could be done by an expert. He wove a tiny weft of the wood of the ambassador's desk into the warp of the wind he'd called up. A sheet of smoke sank to the floor and spread through the room.

He could hear crashing in the offices adjacent to him, and glanced over his shoulder. *Come on,* he mouthed at the weave.

The smoke seemed to find an outlet and went beneath the crack in a wall beside a minibar shaped like a globe of Gergia (the incorrect map). There was a secret door there— if only he could find out how to open it.

Jack yanked on bottles, but nothing worked. He started pulling on cups, and nothing worked. He opened and closed the hatch, and eventually found himself staring at the map.

Someone crashed through the door in the room just behind him.

Jack remembered the nationality of Hēme and looked to Fain. He touched both potential sites of Hēme's hometown —depending on the year of the mating ritual—and felt two invisible little buttons depress beneath his fingers.

A door in the wall swung wide, revealing the main stairwell. Jack stepped inside and closed the door quietly behind him.

14

A LITTLE PLUNGE

"Good evening, fellow dogs," the Klūhman man in black said to the screaming guests. It calmed some down, but increased the volume and pitch of others. Folks ran around, great ribbons and streamers of colors trailing behind them.

"*Chea!*" he shouted.

The room stilled.

"Fellow mongrels, we shall be done here shortly. Your party shall resume tomorrow morning."

A very short, very fat, very red-faced dignitary said, "Kidnapping? A ransom for us from our nations? Because I can tell you if that is the case we take a solemn—"

"Oath to die, yes, dear mutt, I am aware."

"Then what?"

"Assassinate you if you keep asking questions. I'll put you down like the rabid dog you are."

Screeches sounded around the room.

The Klūhman man in black frowned. "Stiller and stiller be, and I may yet let you leave with your lives and posts. Be good little pups on their first prowl."

He nodded to his men, who started moving large containers onto the lifts, the doors closing behind them.

"You can't do that," Dövë said.

Her mother tried to shush her.

The Klūhman man in black put his hand in the doors and opened them again. "Excuse me?"

Dövë stood up to him, shoulders back. "I said you can't do that. We're here to learn from one another."

"So?"

"So you're interrupting."

Frey again tried to shush her.

Dövë ignored her and said, "Well?"

The Klūhman man in black glared. "Silly little hairstyle for a little girl, isn't it? What if I cut it all off?" He pulled out a massive sword.

Frey screamed.

Dövë winced, but did not shrink from him.

"Or forced you to grow it longer?" He danced his left fingers along her braid.

"Whatever," Dövë said.

He then grabbed her by her braid, did some weird sort of magic with the air so that it bulked up his muscles, and threw her clean over the heads of the attendees.

Behind him, a clink sounded.

Half the room turned with the Klūhman man in black to see a young boy with his hand in the proverbial cookie jar, picking through coins.

The other half of the room watched as Dövë crashed into the deceptively deep pool of the fountain.

The Klūhman man in black grabbed up the boy. "Greedy little toad. Let's put you to work." He took him by his ear and forced him all the way to the fountain, getting a lackey to put a sword to his neck. "My friend here has a very sharp sword and will use it on you unless you pick out *every single coin* from this little wishing well."

The boy looked terrified. But he began, first with a little plunge.

Frey did her best to gently, patiently, rescue her daughter, to pull Dövë and her soaking wet dress from the man-made indoor pond.

The Klühman man in black returned to the doors, and they closed behind him.

15

FOR WAR

Black Jack Dawes went through the various rooms on the floors closer to the surface—somewhere around the high thirties, perhaps thirty-fifth?—searching for anything he could use, and anything he could wear. He heard a subtle grinding of stone on stone and the scribbling of a nib in the distance. That gave him enough time to know that a descender had stopped on his floor and someone now headed toward him with a hovering cart that had, by the sound, bumped into the corner of the descender doors.

Jack ducked behind an L-shaped reception booth, using shadows and angles to block whomever approached from seeing as far in as he saw out.

They emerged hauling the largest single slab of brimstone Black Jack had ever seen, even when considering the shipments of brimstone the *Stormsong* had once shipped before the shortage, or even the individual bricks that made up the hidden repository in the school and archive beneath the Nowthin mounts. That great hunk of lightning potentia passed, and behind it was a great vat of quicksilver. And behind that...?

Components for... it looked almost like a wooden arc? A gable for a lodge? A wagon modified to hold giants?

Whatever it was, the three combined told him that *these* weavers, whoever they were and whatever they wanted, had come prepared.

For war.

He backed away from them and snuck back into the stairwell, bolting down into the deeper levels—floors forty-one, forty-three, and on from whence he came—to see what else he'd find deeper in the tap.

16

THE EXCHANGE

"Now," the Klūhman man in black said, "I need the seventeen ambassadors who make up the general council for the Common Realms. Not last year's, this year's."

No one came forward.

Frey eyed Dövë, who looked past the methaqualoin addict in search of her dad. Neither saw whom they needed.

"No dog need die for this," the Klūhman man in black said, "but we have no qualms about cutting through the crowd in order to find you. Beginning with the children." He smiled at Dövë and took his time noticing several other children sitting among the assembled guests.

Outside the windows, steam and smoke rose in the middle distance up the sides of the crater, and various rocks and motes that had crumbled from the wall had caught in the reverse flow of gravity near the tower, just outside the windows, and fell upward.

The Klūhman man in black began reading off names.

Hēme stood.

Frey reached for his arm to tug him down, but missed.

"I am Ambassador Hēme."

Sixteen others slowly rose as well.

"See there?" the leader of the invaders said. "No need for more bloodshed. Come, distinguished dogs."

Hēme cocked his head. He seemed to Frey as a native, unsure of whether the Klūhman in black meant the term as derisive or deferential.

The Klūhman loaded the lot of them into the descenders and rode with them deeper into the tap. They rode in silence until the Klūhman eyed a young, short, skinny, straight-black-haired woman from Soratego.

"Quite the collar and leash," he said to her, nodding at her necklace, her scarf.

She said nothing, only stared forward.

He shrugged at his men.

They shrugged back and rode the up that was down until the doors opened on floor fifty. They all exited, and he led them through a room full of great beanbag chairs, something like a lounge, but with all manner of reclining desks stretched out with inkwells and nibs nearby.

Hēme said, "Fellow pack member or foreign pack member, I can assure you that these tactics will not get you very far. In many of our countries, an ambassadorship is the lowliest role. If we fail to execute our—"

"You think I do not know how Klūhman culture sees an emissary such as yourself?"

Hēme picked at a piece of food in his canine. "I think you might not have considered how widespread that view is."

"Each of you," he said, "was taught a line of a poem. An *ancient* poem. Some might say *the* ancient poem, the song of the bards."

"You weavers use it to cast your spells," Hēme said. "So?"

"So, I will be needing your lines."

The black-haired Sorategan girl said, "Do you not know your own spells?"

The man smiled. "Of course. But you and I both know that the stanzas change, week to week. And they open that strongroom's coffers." He pointed the gunmetal spear he'd wielded the entire time.

Many of the ambassadors, as if seeing it for the first time, turned and noted the strongroom.

"You will give it to me."

"What could you possibly want with the Common Realm strongroom?" Hēme asked. "That won't help you with—"

The man laughed. "It will help me with the seventy-seven million info orders for the ARC, the true currency of the vale. I—Tisyil? What's the exchange?"

A scrawny man came forward and turned a page over in his little notepad. "A quadrillion dollars for earthbound, fourteen thousand cubic tons of corality, a ton of liquid Sicilian. Those are the core controvertible currencies."

The man smiled. "He does the math, what do I know about this? But... and correct me if I'm wrong, but I'd say that sounds like *a whole caboodle of monies and noodles*, wouldn't you?"

17

A SWINGING CAGE

She probably should have ignored the Klūhman in black, but Dövë found herself as angry as The Pit. She vented about this to another little girl, an Æ†eœuoƐ˥ian girl named zæ†eœuoƐ˥ɥæ†eœuoƐ˥shæ†eœuoƐ˥cĥhy, which meant "flirtatious gesture," though the girl insisted on being called Zæ. She and Dövë had struck up a friendship over being locked up together—and being among the children in the crowd whom the Klūhman in black had threatened to "cut through." Presumably with one of those swords.

"I want to get at him," Dövë said.

"I found some slugs in that fountain," said Zæ. "Pretty big ones. We could put that in his chair."

"Better idea. Get it first."

Zæ took her time navigating the rather large ballroom in her thick, heavy dress; it had been crafted of layers upon layers of bold dyed doily lace so that the final result was hundreds of layers deep of patterns upon patterns upon patterns in all the main colors of the rainbow. When she moved, it moved in fractals like a kaleidoscope. But damn was the thing heavy for a little girl.

She got over there, however, and dug some slugs. "Let's put it in his chair," she said.

But before Dövë could consent to that, she felt her mind overpowering her senses—as if she could reach out and touch everything in the room with her thoughts, and her thoughts would become the thoughts of the objects and the air and space around them. As if all her eleventh-month full sentences and her fifteen-month bilingual capacity and her second-year literacy and her fourth-year move from reading all the children's books to reading all the classics had simply... boiled over. And now those thoughts could reach out and touch almost anything.

She reached out with her mind and thought—to the slug —*flying*.

It flew.

She thought *strafing*.

It navigated around the perimeter of the room, out of sight of almost everyone.

She thought *descending*.

It did so toward the Klūhman in black's favorite drinking cup, the one with the handmade metal straw. It was harder than she thought it would be to aim, but she accomplished it. The slug splashed water when it hit.

The Klūhman in black returned briefly, took a sip from his drink, and tasted the slug. He spat it out, freaked, and locked eyes with Dövë.

"*You*," he said.

"Me?" Dövë asked.

"You did this," he said.

"How?"

Frey said, "No, no, no."

The man called up the metal in the rafters, bent it to his will into a swinging cage, and hung the little girl within it.

Frey was sobbing.

"Let that be a lesson to you children: stay out of my way."

18

'I WILL COUNT TO THREE DOGS

Black Jack bypassed the other floors in the stairwell and, following the faint sound of voices, emerged on the fiftieth. He ducked down behind a series of long, low, wood-skirted coffee tables that followed a series of wavy benches all throughout the hall. Other than his hat and the yellow stone within, he was still naked as a skinned skinny snake.

From a crouched position, he heard the dickering of the Klūman man in black over what exactly they had gathered to do. He heard the arguing with the seventeen ambassadors, and heard when the man in black asked for the poem to the Common Realm strongroom.

Jack then pulled out his Crowfoot and pointed the sharpened leg bone toward the rest of the room.

Hēme, he could see from his vantage, was standing up to the man.

"I don't know the rest of their lines," the ambassador said, "but I can tell you I won't tell you mine. And without mine, you can't open the rest. You need every stanza."

"I will count from no dogs to a three-legged dog. One leg. Two Leg. Three legs."

Hēme laughed. "Guess you'll have to kill me."

So the Klūhman in black did. He called up lightning quicker than almost any weave Black Jack had seen and blew a bright and crispy hole through Black Jack's wife's boss.

Jack's breath died in his throat, hissed clean out of him.

The other ambassadors screamed.

The little fat man and the young woman also refused to share their stanzas. So, angry, the Klūhman in black smote them too. He smote them all with sky fire. Seventeen dead.

This wasn't a kidnapping.

This was an assassination.

Naked, Black Jack booked it out of there, hitting several things along the way.

19

OFFWORLDER

A few of the men in the room full of seventeen dead ambassadors perked up at the sound of Black Jack's departure, including the redcrown and the redcrown's son. With a nod from the Klūhman in black, they bolted toward the stairwell. But they did not find Black Jack Dawes in the direction in which they pursued him: up toward the party.

It took them a long time to consider going the other way: deeper even than floor fifty.

"What are we going to do?" the offworlder named Tisyil asked.

"You get to cracking and we'll wait for Inquisitors," Krif Tayfyet said.

"How are they gonna be any help?" Tisyil asked. "The water barrier will still lock down."

"You will see. Get cracking."

20

INHERITANCE

Sfòne stood beneath Dövë's cage. Frey had asked him to watch her while she dealt with some of the other survivors. The upside of being absolutely, positively horrified at your daughter's fate in a gibbet was... you know... knowing she wasn't going anywhere.

Sfòne and Dövë made light conversation as folks went to and fro.

"Why are you here?" Dövë asked.

"Your mother."

"I know you want to date her," Dövë said.

"Uh."

"It's obvious."

"We can talk about that if you—"

"Not now," Dövë said. "That's not a why. That's a for whom."

"I... am..." He looked around the room, but no one but Dövë was paying attention. "I am related to the Klūhman in black."

"He put you up to this?"

"No. He... he's my uncle. He's been keeping me down."

"How?"

"Well... my mother died. And she left an inheritance to me that would pass to him, her brother, if I didn't make it. So he found a way to keep me here when she died. Sort of wait me out."

"How'd she die?" Dövë asked.

"Suspiciously."

Dövë waited.

He looked around again. "He's somehow rigged it so that the interest from that salary goes into my expense account here so that I'm not really making any more money, just drawing against the interest of my mother's estate. A pittance. Enough to eat on. Most of the time."

"Describe your mother to me," Dövë said.

Sfòne described his mother in vivid detail to the girl in the makeshift hanging cage.

21

FASHIRALS

Down in the second-to-lowest level of the tap—the floor right above the roof that made up the glass observation deck that hovered sixty feet or so above the great lava well—a couple of the Klūhman invaders (and their various compadres from Gergia and elsewhere in The Vale) arrived by a freight descender. The Common Realms had often used it to haul in mammoths for indoor circuses or military equipment for lectures on international defense.

The invaders, however, squeezed out an enormous creature that filled most of the descender's cubic footage. It was see-through, like a column of ebbing water with bubbles working through it, and with surface tension that now and again seemed to form legs or a head or a rolling wave. They moved it as one might move a tiger or an elephant before the main event. No whips or open flame, swords sheathed. They pushed the creature forward using long pillows, feather ticklers, and cotton-swab-tipped long poles.

"Beneath the catwalk so he touches most of the floor," said a man in green with a bulbous wart on his earlobe.

This floor featured all manner of grey stone fashirals. Fashirals that warmed the floors of the tap, fashirals that controlled the descenders, fashirals meant to control water and air and especially the reverse flow of gravity that vented the heat around the tap toward the surface. Near indestructible, that one, judging by the casings.

But most of that existed atop a large black metal catwalk that hovered on a sort of second tier or loft above the rest. The space beneath the catwalk was mostly empty.

They coaxed the monster beneath it, slowly and surely, to flatten out so that it took up almost the entire floor.

The floor that made up the ceiling of the observation deck.

Above the lava.

22

IN CASE OF LAVA FLOW
BREACH

Stricken with fear for his wife, his daughter, that jackass hooked on methaqualoin, and the little girls who had played strings, Black Jack hustled lower and lower into the tap. Away from the party. Away from the surface and the murdered seventeen.

He came out in a room that was empty apart from some old tables and bookshelves. Dust had collected and parchment sat strewn about. Perhaps the occupants had recently switched floors? Or buildings? But the books remained behind foggy, swirly glass, left alone and unattended by whoever had once used them for research or pleasure or in order to make them a better person.

He looked around for some sort of non-woven weapon, as there was no guarantee he could swipe some brimstone from these assassins. He saw no sword. No polearm. He didn't get the sense that anything other than the desperation of throwing books would help him in this room. No gyrocompasses. Nothing.

Then, on the wall, he saw a little lever behind a

crystalline encasement. On it were these hand-painted
words:

I N CASE OF LAVA FLOW BREACH
    OR SEISMIC EVENT
    SHATTER CRYSTAL,
TWIST KNOB,
AND PULL LEVER.

J ack punched through the thin crystal frame and
sounded a massive alarm. Ice and water began
sleeting from sapphire veins in the ceiling to cool
nonextant lava.

A clarion horn went off, a ship in the fog.

Jack slid over sleet to get to the window, where he
looked up to the boardwalks and bridges fifty floors above
him. Tiny dots in the high and far distance grew wings: he
had called a great team of bomberos on iceagles.

23

THROUGH ICENESS

As the Klūhman in black sat freezing in the indoor sleeting, he picked up his own handheld onyx gyrocompass. He rotated it and then called on an open channel. "Oily Oscar, you there?"

Oily Oscar was quietly watching regional security channels in case they realized the stables had been barricaded and how empty, for a party, the pull-through beneath the valet awning had become. Now he shot forward and picked up the dark compass. "Krif Tayfyet."

"Need you to use the ice compass at the front desk."

"For...?"

"Call off the bomberos. Check the gapequill."

Oily Oscar looked left and saw the long writing quill recording the functions of various fashirals that ran the bureaucratic defenses, alarms, and basic functions. In big, bold letters (the fashiral had used the massive-nibbed quill that was reserved for emergencies), the scroll said:

. . .

L AVA FLOW OR SEISMIC EVENT

It listed the floor.

"Okay." Oily Oscar picked up the ice compass, which moved to an unknown music of unseen spheres in various universes. Oily spoke *through iceness*, the form and universal genre and class and essence of all ice, actual and potential, and, calibrated to a near-range of this world, he picked up the bomberos on the iceness frequency.

"Come in, bomberos. Come in, bomberos."

The captain answered. "Hoi, who speaketh?"

"Security of the Hollow Needle tap, core station and business of the Common Realms."

"On thee hath fallen this unforeseen disaster and sapped thy life? Rained you are and long to resign the boon of existence?"

"No," Oily said. "False alarm."

"False?"

"False. Happening all evening, honestly. Wondering if it's just the high number of guests concentrated on one floor during off-peak hours."

Silence on the other end.

Oily watched the iceagles pause in air.

"Proceed thy fireless deed in silence and go forth on thy bold path of daring."

They turned and flew away.

After a minute, on the onyx compass, the Klūhman in black said, "Good."

"Thanks, boss."

A moment. "Krif Oscar?"

"Yeah?" Oily said.

"On what floor does that gapequill say the alarm sounded?"

Oily Oscar looked again at the words below LAVA FLOW OR SEISMIC EVENT.

"Fifty."

24

BRIMSTONE BUILLION

lack Jack, too, saw the iceagles pause in air. "Little birds," he said in the midst of the indoor sleeting storm. "Little birds, I found some worms for you."

They flew away.

"Shit, shit, shit."

Two sounds: a door smashing open and thunder.

Two sights: a red-headed young man and sapphire-veined spider lightning among the raining and sleeting and icing and snowing. Lightning jumped droplets, catching the quickest route to Black Jack.

Who—on reflex—had shot up off the wet and into the little desk's wooden cubby. Dammit. He hated fighting naked. And wet. It's *very, very* difficult.

CRACK.

POW.

Lightning struck overhead. Between blasts he crouch-ran toward the next desk, splashing and sliding. Lightning cracked behind him, a spear of hellfire poking hole after hole in the great glass wall of the tap so that the open air and its reverse gravity beyond whistled at them.

He snuck around the bookshelves and tiptoed on wet rug behind the red-headed young man with the backpack and the smaller satchel on his shoulder.

Lightning struck out from the boy—*crack, crack, crack*—poking holes in bookshelves and backpacks.

Then Black Jack—the nakeder, larger man—jumped on the young man.

The young man swung in reaction. His fist hit Jack, knocking the Crowfoot free. The two swung around each other in orbit. Jack punched at the kid's stylet. A fossilized bit of straw. Or hay? The kid dropped it, then suddenly realized his assailant was naked. He hesitated, shocked.

Jack landed a punch on the kid's jaw.

The kid punched back.

Blow traded blow.

But the kid was well trained in boxing, and Jack...?

Jack was a piece of work. His lip got bloodied, his chest checked. Back and forth they went, running after one another, dodging, each trying to pick up their own stylet. On top of shelves, on top of desks, sliding over the wet rugs. Until Jack, seeing an opportunity through the murk in some kind of artifact, spear-tackled the kid and drove him backward. He assumed the kid would hit some sort of vase and get TKO'd.

It turned out to be an obsidian spire gifted to the Common Realm ambassadors in the name of diplomatic solutions from the golden hall of the panther king. The twisted spire had come unrigged and now angled out rather than up. The kid's back hit the thing and it speared him through.

"Yeah, good," the kid whispered. And died.

The sleeting fashiral turned off.

Jack was freezing cold. He could see his breath.

Through some very awkward maneuvers, the details of which I'll spare you, he got the outer clothes off the boy. None of them fit. The boy was, let's face it, half his size. Jack tried to rip them, but with a big hole through the tunic, it was no use.

Instead he opened the small satchel. Inside was a book of matches from some bar named *The Ace Hotel,* tipped in sulfur (more brimstone), but... he seemed to remember matches being hard to find in Gergia, again due to the brimstone shortage. He closed the bag and put it over his naked shoulders, then squeezed out a good deal of water from the brim of his hat. Then he checked the backpack the kid wore, same as the rest of them.

Inside lay dozens of brimstone bullion bricks and three different kinds of compasses, including the onyx kind like the one he'd left with his driver, Fetch, the "standard black" communication device of most of the western world. He went back to grab his Crowfoot and deposited the fossilized hay stylet in the bag.

"Yeah, good," Black Jack whispered to himself. He'd never killed a kid before. Had never wanted to.

"Yeah, good," he said, burning the kid's last words on his mind.

Not much older than Dövë.

"Yeah, good."

He looked down to the door from whence the kid had come and saw the descenders. He looked back to the kid. He didn't want to do what he knew he needed to do to send the assailants over the edge. His own voice whined at the thought of it.

"Yeah... yeah, good."

25

BODY OF HIS SON

The lift opened before the lounging brimstone weavers and the redcrown and Tayfyet turned to see what cowardly little rodent the redcrown's son had killed. The cowardly little rodent that had escaped the party and nearly spoiled them with some measure of lava alarm.

Instead what they found was a hole in the boy's chest and, in blood across the white stone, the words: *Now I too have brimstone, bomberos.*

The redcrown screamed and ran to grab the body of his fallen son.

26

REYGLOW

Black Jack had used a deck to keep the door pried open while he staged the scene, however much he hated doing it, and when he was done he had climbed atop an emergency suspended marble descender box. The subsequent ride back up to the fiftieth floor had terrified him—no railings, nothing to keep him away from the feeling of *speed*, and the empty carriages in the descender deadspace moving up and down and somehow staying in their lanes.

Now, from his vantage point, he could see little, but he heard into the descender shaft as the redcrown shouted.

"Krif Lūwof," Tayfyet said.

Black Jack could see the owner of that voice just beyond the darkened slots above the doors, just out into the light of the room. He counted two, plus the dead one, then shifted position and saw seven more through the vents.

The redcrowned Lūwof screamed. *"My boy!"*

"Krif Lūwof," Tayfyet said.

The redcrown wept and hollered and howled.

The room and descender shaft and marble box grew

black as pitch as Tayfyet drew all of the light in the room up into a great warp—a loom of light—before him.

The crowd, which had been mumbling and muttering and moving to see, stilled.

As did the redcrown.

"You will be able to find him," Tayfyet said, "and burn his soul to The Pit." He released the light back to the room, calling off the lightweave. "But..."

Black Jack wondered: Where had these Klūhmen come from? Reyglow? The accent and use of brimstone seemed to suggest it.

27

THE RECEIVING END

Fifty yards away, Frey sat holding Dövë, shaking her head and smiling.

"What?" Sfòne asked.

"Jack."

"Your husband? What about him?"

She giggled to herself.

"What?" He was massaging his black palm.

"He's the only one I know so desperate to help somebody that he'd hurt somebody else that badly in the process." She giggled again.

Dövë joined her.

"Why are you giggling?" Sfòne asked. "It's a terrible thing, terrible thing to giggle at." Then he looked at the attackers, who had noticed her giggling. "Quiet. You'll get us killed."

"Because," Frey said, "it's the first time I've been on the receiving end of his help since I became pregnant with Dövë."

28

DUMPED HIS MEMORIES

For a storyweaver as tenured as Black Jack Dawes—neither the highest ranking nor the most powerful, but *tenured* with the scars to show it—it didn't take long to make another brimstone compass keyed to his own loci, though it took a lot of one the twelve brimstone bullion bars in order to do it. That left eleven. More ammo than he would ever need for one fight, and not anywhere near enough for the long slog ahead he feared.

Just to be on the safe side, he took one of the eleven bars from the little ammo backpack and put it in with the matchbook from the Ace Hotel. You never knew when your bags might get separated.

The palm-sized compass looked identical in form to the others, but with the added benefit of showering sparks between the whirling wheels upon whirling wheels. A tiny circus gyro. Yeah, it was costly and risky to make, but he needed the compass because he needed to access his loci, his private section of the archive, and to remember as much as he could.

He quickly stored memories in his mind palace: the

men in the elevator, their numbers, the names Krif Lūwof, Oily Oscar, and Krif Tayfyet. He compiled what he remembered of the bags of brimstone bricks—each had one and, good gravy, that seemed like a lot of cash to burn on this one tower. It was the sort of thing he'd expect if they fully planned to assassinate every dignitary in the place, quick as they'd cut through the entire battalion of guards. But weavers—storied or otherwise—could do that.

He dumped the rest of his memories.

Then he looked out the windows and saw, beyond the whirling winds and steam and smoke beyond the anti-gravity buffer, through the mirage waves of the heat, the black stone of the wall. Onyx.

Out of curiosity, he used his mind's eye and mind's body to journey through the Somnolory mindscape through his mind's own backdoor into the part of the archive that connected to theories on compasses. They were stored, those ideas, in little clay jars he had to break with a bell hammer. He searched by material until he found onyx. Searched through onyx compasses in the archival catalog until he found ways of boosting signals. Sometimes you could make a general directive in the compasses with enough power—as with his newly fashioned brimstone one. But you used generic stone ones to communicate hyper-locally, and you broadcasted your thoughts toward someone specific using, for instance, the brimstoneness of the compass to contact the brimstoneness of the compass fashioned by the person you were trying to reach. Moving through the narrative essence of the logoi of both compasses and the logos in which they participated. Ways of boosting existed, but he didn't know much about onyx.

Turned out, a mine and a massive wall of onyx would

do it. So he decided to get as low in the wall as possible, surrounded by as much as possible.

That meant the tip of the tap.

He searched once more on the empty floor for clothes and found none. He really wished at times like this that he'd chosen woodweaving as his first weaving tree: it was otherwise very, very difficult to manifest clothing out of thin air. He hopped back onto the descender's roof in case someone joined him from another floor; he didn't want the doors to open on his naked ass. Armed with the Crowfoot, he reached with his foot to the floor assignment quill, scribbled the note for the floor with his toes, then took off down the shaft after the doors had closed.

He met no problems, though he heard some Klūhman—*māit, krif pwar runga: hol mpet mpeyye!*—on the floor above.

This floor was silent. Everything was made of great, thick glass. Spare outlines of furniture and walls. A few foodstuffs and bottles of wine obscured the view, but otherwise you could see everything. He felt like he might fall down—real down—into the great roiling, boiling lava pool.

He noticed the way the reverse flow of gravity power-steamed, power-smoked the sides of the walls, most of which were onyx.

He squinted to see which side had the most onyx, went over there and thought of the *onyxness* of the generic compass he had received from the pierced boy, the child of the redcrown Krif Lūwot. And then he began to broadcast using the tap shaft—the very crater itself. Broadcasting as a giant insect's antennae broadcast to the hive.

29

REDCROWN

"Come in, watchmen. Come in, sentries."

"Who is that?" Krif Lūwof asked Krif Tayfyet, lifting his own generic onyx compass.

"This is Hollow Needle sending out a distress signal. The tap has been breached by well-armed, well-trained, extremely dangerous weavers who have taken hostage the entirety of the collected ambassadors of the Common Realms."

Krif Lūwof growled and whispered, "The man who killed my son. Where is he?"

The blue-suited, brass-buttoned guard lookalike said, "He's using a signal booster. There's no chance otherwise."

Krif Lūwof looked between the blue-suit and Krif Tayfyet.

Who looked out at the crowd, searching

Krif Lūwof looked past his master's gaze through the window and saw the onyx vein. *The observatory,*" he said. "There's even more onyx down below. He's pooling the onyx like a bucket of power." He was off toward the descender.

Krif Tayfyet said, "Lūwof!"

The redcrown ignored him as he and another went off down the descender.

30

THUNDERSTRUCK

The local watcher thought it a prank. "What do you want to do?" he asked the headmistress of the watcher station.

She shrugged.

But then an extreme static—which they never heard on the clear-as-a-bell compasses—erupted and squelched the compass's voice so that the tinnitus rang out in their ears. Then *crack! pow!*

Thunder had struck.

The watcher said, "We gotta call in someone."

The headmistress nodded. "Send in that sentry, the knight who doesn't use his sword anymore."

The girls all laughed at that.

31
NEAR THE TIP

The Knight Who Didn't Use His Sword Anymore was named Terence Thomas Tryban-Trevor. They called him 4T or Forty. He was fifty-five and fat, Forty. Forty was in a fast-food joint. Not that kind of fast-food joint. The Gergian kind—the kind most planets in The Vale unconcerned about post-electric technology had. This one boasted a line of some thirty miniature furnaces warming little personal-sized clay pots full of special vittles. People actually hiked halfway up the foothills that rose above the Hollow Needle in order to get their food. Forty wasn't there for that. These guys baked. These guys baked *good*. He was here for the lard bread. They put waaaaay too little prosciutto in it, waaaay too little cheese, but tons and tons of lard. Just gobs of the stuff.

And that's why Forty was fat.

"Come in, Ser Terence."

He winced—he hated his first name—and picked up his compass while the family-sized portion of lard bread warmed. "Yeah?"

"You still en route to the Hollow Needle?"

"Yeah..." He eyed the dripping, drizzling, sizzling fat. "Still got that stray horse I need to bring in."

"We got some kid telling us the entire building's been taken over by anarchists or something. Do you mind taking a pesky?"

"Sure, lovey dove."

"Quit."

"Should I bring in the stray?"

The woman on the line spat. "You can't handle an extra horse for another fifteen minutes, Ser Forty?"

He put away his compass and took his lard bread from the guy at the counter. "Eating for two," he said to the baker, patting the belly.

"You and your fat baby?" the baker replied.

"Twins."

"Mazel tov."

"What's that mean?" Forty asked.

"Means good fortune or something on my mom's home world, how do I know?" He flipped some sourdough.

Forty shrugged and went outside and fed a good portion of the bread to both horses. His gobbled it down; the stray spat it out.

"Prissy little..."

He heave-hoed himself up onto his own horse, cinched the reins of the stray around the back of the saddle, and started off for the fifteen-minute journey down to the tap. But first, seeing as he was high atop the foothills that overlooked the Hollow Needle, he grew curious and simply walked the horses to the railing on the edge of the very cliff that held the fast-food joint. He peered down the cliff, down the foothills, down all the way to the crater at the bottom into which the Hollow Needle's tap had been constructed.

Down near the tip, down near the glass observatory he knew was there but couldn't quite see, he thought amid the smoke and steam and lava that he saw flashes of lightning.

32

RAGE OF A DEAD SON

Down on the observatory deck, Krif Lūwof had exploded upon the naked Black Jack with hellfire and fury. Ball lightning shot out of the end of his stylet—which was his saber—and, having been dodged by Jack, hit the other wall like a plasma ball hitting glass.

It did not explode. It didn't blast holes as the great bolts had upstairs in the dusty book room. Instead it bounced and then, like a plasma ball or Tesla coil, writhed spider legs of lightning off toward the other glass, bright blue where it touched, closer and closer to whatever ground it could find for discharge.

This close to the lava, Black Jack became painfully aware of his lava warmers. He hoped he was not *too* close. He saw through a glass cabinet to Krif Lūwof on the other side, shooting another ball, which bounced and did something similar to the first, only closer to the glass floor.

Aware of the boundaries of the glass battlefield they occupied, Krif Lūwof tried to run to the other side to get an angle on Black Jack. Instead he hit his knee on a nearly invisible cabinet.

The naked storyweaver took the second afforded by Krif Lūwof's knee to sprint around the other way, sliding when he could. The faint outlines of various glass furniture pieces and tools passed him by. Ball after ball chased him, and a couple of bolts as well, which fizzled in the air.

He glanced back. Krif Lūwof was somehow reassimilating the ball lightning into brimstone bullion. The rage of a dead son in his pulsing temple and molars gnashing, he blasted bolt after bolt at Black Jack's head.

Jack ducked and ran for the lift.

The way was blocked off by a great spray of spider lightning.

Black Jack slid beneath that, a couple of static shocks hitting him like firecrackers, and on through to the other side, where he kicked open the stairwell door.

33

GLOWING HOLES

Up he ran one floor to the fashirals. Something billowy and bubbly writhed below the catwalk, but he ignored it. He heard voices in the other room, drunk Klūhmen.

The pen on the lift scribbled.

Think, think, think.

He looked back at the lift shaft from whence he'd come. Could he open it without waiting for a descender to come?

He called up a warp of brimstone, called up a weft of the limestone floor. Wove a lightning-powered battering ram, a spell he'd used often. He shot it at the silent door. Hammerfell and stone doors hit the far back wall of the shaft and plummeted up into the abyss that led to the front office.

Followed by silence.

Then a massive noise in the nearby room.

Black Jack had seconds. He ran to the edge of the lift and felt immediately woozy from the potential speed of the freefall up. He called up another warp of lightning and then searched the room for something to use.

The water heater fashiral.

He said the word. Water shot through the spigot and attached to the talons of his Crowfoot. He stitched, froze the lightning bolt, which he inverted—the splintering branches of light forming a wedge grapple in the door—and slid down the bolt toward the point of origin, static raising his arm hairs. Terribly jagged rope met naked body, only hat and bag in the way, and cuts appeared all over him. On that frozen upside-down lightning tree, the shaft pulling him upward, he looked down and saw dozens of Klūmen—and Krif Lūwof himself, staring.

They pulled out stylets and pointed at him and wall and bolt.

He swung on the bolt, which creaked and crackled.

The shaft around him exploded with light and thunder from the Klūhmen.

He swung toward the other door. Inches away, his bolt melted—an unraveling cast by a moron above.

Spider lightning unfrozen blasted from Black Jack's point of origin back toward its splinters, hitting ten men at once. That diffused, it wouldn't kill a one of them, but it knocked them back.

That didn't matter to Jack, because his rope had shot free from his grip and now he fell up.

Five.

Ten.

Fifteen floors.

Before he called a weft of stone from the wall, barely slowing his descent before slamming face-first into it. Snapped his nose and sent blood gushing forth. His hands snagged the edge of a space—a little tunnel or duct—between lift doors somewhere between floors seventy and seventy-one.

Krif Lūwof stared up at him, counting floors. Then he shot bolt after bolt.

Black Jack, blinded by the flashbangs as well as the tears from his bloody nose, and with barely room to hang with one hand, pulled up the same weaving—stone and lightning—that he'd used above. He blew the door back.

Flashes around him from Krif Luwof. It was hard to aim lightning from that distance.

The door wasn't a lift door. It was a tiny intake valve on some sort of ventilation shaft. It bounced off the wall behind, came back, caught the strap of Jack's brimstone bullion bag, and fell up the shaft, carrying his lightning ammo with it.

Jack screamed a cussword as he pulled himself into the vent, grateful the other bag remained in hand, hat on head, stone in hat, and that he'd had the wherewithal to slip one brimstone bullion brick into the bag he still held.

Now what? he thought as he squat-walked through the air intake vents.

Some of the exit holes before him showed what was happening in the room below, and he saw Krif Lūwof sprint through the door, call up lightning, weave flame and a spray of his spit into it, and shoot, rapid-fire, holes into the thin passage. It sounded like ratchets uncoiling.

A thousand smoking, glowing holes appeared where the lightning had pierced. One was just beside Jack's knee, another inches from his face. He pulled out his one last brick of brimstone and armed himself with the Crowfoot.

Krif Lūwof walked up to the vent and turned his saber into a glowing torch by calling light. Almost every weaver could do that, but few true lightweavers existed because most thought lightweaving impotent, trivial, even childish.

But Black Jack had seen Niran—chief lightweaver—do things with light that Black Jack could never comprehend.

Lūwof's light beam swept the holes twenty feet ahead, making a thousand tiny spotlights. Several hundred spotlights fifteen feet ahead. More ten feet from him.

Black Jack pursed his lips to call forth brimstone.

"Krif Lūwof?" a compass said.

Lūwof stopped sweeping and picked up the compass. "What?"

"Get down here. We may have a security problem."

Krif Lūwof scoffed. He listened closely instead of sweeping the light beam. Then he turned and left through the door he'd come through, and Black Jack heard him board the descender.

Only then did Black Jack pant in and out and in and out.

34

ICECOMPASS

Ser Forty rode slowly. He brought both horses up to the edge of the building, tied off, scanned over the single floor that rose above the platform, walked to the chest-high latticed railing over on the edge, and peered all the way down to the fiery abyss below. He didn't see the lightning. Perhaps the lava made for weird weather?

He looked around and saw the steam-smoke circle rising around and above the reverse gravity flow buffer. Checked horses and walked to the front door.

Locked.

The main desk man emerged. Oily... but he bore a smile and waved his hand as if to say, *Come in, brother, come on in.*

Ser Forty tried. The door clattered against its locks.

The oily man cracked it and said, "Good even, watchman."

"Even. The watchman dispatcher heard a call of emergency for a lava flow? Seismic?"

"Sure, one second. See that oily paint on both sides of the walkway? Watch that, we just painted—wouldn't want you to get any on your boots. Stick to the white stone path to the front desk and don't venture any further and you won't get any on you." He pursed his lips looking at the paint. A bead of sweat.

"Oh, thanks. Yeah, new boots," Ser Forty said.

The oily man nodded. "Yeah, we've had those alarms going off about once a month. Reverse gravity shield needs tweaking."

"Mind if I check your distress signals?"

The oily man led Ser Forty behind the desk and pointed to a row of gapequills working on their self-winding scrolls. He then sat back down to a complicated card game called dökë sfïŷi—just him versus the cards on the table.

Forty saw the emergency signals and took note of floor fifty. "Distress call on the local icecompass line?"

The oily man tensed. "Some prank. It's fine."

Forty eyed him.

The man went back to his cards.

Forty looked left at the quills and noticed another set showing errors in the descender shafts as well as some sort of electrical disturbance on the observation deck. Perhaps the flashes?

"Mind if I peek at your descenders?"

"Paint's wet there too. Stick to the white stone."

Wet paint. Forty didn't buy it, would walk where he wanted if he so wanted, but he nodded.

Around the corner he found a dozen or so very normal doors that hid the various descenders. Nothing to warrant a distress signal. No smoke, no fight, no fire.

35

CANCELING THE WEAVE

Black Jack had hopped down through the ducts weakened by the lightning holes. He had checked for bad guys, clothes, more brimstone ammo. Found none. He'd run to the large windows and looked up. He had watched as the knight descended the hillside with two horses. Had seen him looking over the edge.

He watched the knight come down the hillside, inspect the front. After a while, he saw Ser Forty coming back out again.

Stay! he wanted to shout.

He needed help rescuing Frey and Dövë. He pounded on the glass and started to call up a weave that would shatter or reposition it.

The door was kicked in by a brimstone weaver. Another brimstone weaver shouted and pointed at Jack.

Jack whirled, shooting lightning.

One man ducked. The second fired at Jack.

Their bolts met in midair.

Thunder hit thunder. Wave interference ensured that

what had been two deafening sounds turned instead to the concussive pressure of a room awash in silence.

Sparks everywhere.

The two men shot at Jack.

Jack shot back.

A cupboard of brandy exploded. Blood-red contents hit the plaster wall. Glass shards went everywhere.

A table exploded.

Chairs.

Great jagged carbon scoring etched eldritch black labyrinths on white-painted walls.

Jack got off a bit of ball lightning with a clean *half* of the brimstone bullion brick and hit the second man square in the chest. Blue white explosion where the man had been. That gave Jack enough time to run beneath a roundtable with a great lazy Susan in the middle.

The other man hopped on the lazy Susan and started walking around the table, blasting holes in it.

Holes that marked the floor where Jack had been.

Once.

Twice.

Thrice.

Until Jack—surrounded by the legs of chairs and barely shielded overhead by the sparse table-turned-termite-ridden-cedar-stock—had nowhere to go but the last slice of table pie.

The brimstone weaver said, "Fire razes forest." He called up a massive amount of brimstone.

Jack called up the rest of his last full brick on his own, then called up the wood in all of the chairs around them in an even fifty-fifty weave, wove it, and threw it into the table.

Instant ash and cinder and charcoal.

Jack had no brimstone left, but he didn't need to look to know that the man above had turned into a black carbon sculpture of his former self.

"Ground to sky lightning," he said to the dead man. He went to the window and saw Ser Forty uncinching his horse, moving to leave. "Nope, nope, nope."

The window before Black Jack had spiderweb fractures in the glass from the firefight. He turned and saw the table with the body of the man now fused to it in a sort of charcoal sculpture. Not dense enough, but it was a start. He looked up once more at the knight's walkway high above and out from the exterior of the building. He judged the trajectory the reverse flow of the tap would give it, if the falling rocks sign had been any indication. Then he got behind the charcoal sculpture, his lava gloves protecting him from the heat, and shoved it as hard as he could toward the window.

But as he thought about it, he realized the reverse flow of gravity would probably make it arc up and then down the other side of the building, or land far away from the knight like the rocks. A parabolic trajectory. He looked to the other side of the floor and saw that the lightning had damaged that window too. So he got on the other edge of the giant charred table and heaved, hoping the casters still worked.

It took a moment to get some momentum. He pushed and pushed, high knees the whole way, until he got to a full sprint. He shoved the table straight into the massive pane of glass, which exploded, and the entire thing shot out the window.

Up.

It would arc over the building soon.

He ran back to the first window, called up the pane as if

to weave it, set it aside whole, canceling the weave, and poked his head out of the hole.

The great burnt corpse of the brimstone weaver and the table shot into view high in the sky behind the tap and the tap's first floor as gravity reasserted itself.

36

ONYX COMPASS

Ser Forty continued toward his horse, uncinched it, and had just turned toward the othern when high in the air, some great black thing shot up and over and came plummeting down toward him. He started running backward with his horse lead as the black mass fell.

Toward the stray.

It crushed the horse, poor soul, breaking its body and ending its life.

Forty noted the remains of the poor soul scorched and fused to the table, eyes burned out. He saddled quickly, and by the time he'd turned the horse to get some reinforcements, lightning broke nearby windows.

Lightning directed at him.

He kicked the horse into a racing gallop, pulling out his onyx compass as he went.

"I need as many watchmen as are in the area to come to the tap RIGHT THIS SECOND! Hollow Needle, now! Take thresholds. They attacked an officer with excessive force."

He rode and rode and rode up the hills, lightning trailing him, rode all the way to the shelter of the pines. From there he could see the weavers in the leftern windows of the floors closest to the entrance, eyeing him.

37

TSÆT

It took the better part of an hour, but knights and some lower weavers and various guards and bowmen arrived. Ser Forty quickly filled in his captain, TsætteœuoꞀy. He called the man Captain Tsæt because ÆteœuoƐlian had too many damnable syllables and vowels in it for quick talk. The ÆteœuoƐlians liked it that way. Forty did not. He'd once had an ÆteœuoƐlian conversation about a rainbow appearing over his mother's coffin with an ÆteœuoƐlian guest whom he had welcomed into his home for some Ivrian tourism. The story about his mother's coffin grew difficult immediately, for the ÆteœuoƐlian word for rainbow was shæteœuoƐlthæteœuoƐlræteœuoƐl hwæteœuoƐlchhyæteœuoƐl and the ÆteœuoƐlian word for coffin was yæteœuoƐlyæteœuoƐlg thæteœuoƐlgæteœuoƐlthæteœuoƐl. It took the better part of five minutes just to set up the story, and by then their coffee had come.

So he'd long ago learned to call his captain Tsæt.

When Forty finished, Tsæt scowled. "What kind of screwup is this? I'll take over."

"It's the kind I'm not gonna let you take over, Tsæt. Some really bad dudes in there."

Tsæt grimaced. He didn't like Forty's nickname for him.

38
TAFFY

After Jack saw the horse crushed and the knight running away chased by lightning bolts, he shouted, "Welcome to the great Common Realms diplomacy ball!"

He spat, then looked back into the room where the other body lay. It wore enough that Jack could strip him and use his clothes and no longer be quite as naked. The stuff fit tightly around his slowly growing beer belly (a bit of padding on an otherwise distinguished physique), but less naked was less naked. And the shoes fit.

Then he rifled through the huge bag the man had carried.

Inside was a tiny, curious, cooing little hydrazite monster—a baby—and a series of little vials full of what Jack was absolutely certain contained volatile faeflame.

"Good gravy, Miss Maybe," Jack said.

He refilled his empty brimstone satchel with a couple of the bricks that had been left over from the foe's attack, then he shouldered the satchel with the hydrazite and faeflame.

He picked up the man's onyx compass and made himself known to those listening on the other end. "Hey ho there, Tayfyet. Mind if I call you Taffy? Laughy Taffy?"

39

FAEFLAME

K rif Tayfyet looked slapped. He tried to regain his composure before his men noticed, but many did. He had counted on knights, on guards, on the descenders, the ambassadors refusing passwords, on weavers gathering for an assault on the tap, whiny hostages, betrayals from his men, on the involvement of The Bigwigs, and even militaries of the nations represented.

But one rogue had snuck out, and now he had no idea where to place him in this massive game of Hollow Needle chess that had been set in motion.

Hidden chess pieces scared him.

"You have a nickname for me," Krif Tayfyet said, "but I have none for you, Mister..."

"You don't want to guess? All right, okay," the man who had killed Tayfyet's men said.

"Someone who grew up in a military home?" Krif Tayfyet asked.

"Nah."

"Knights errant stories?"

Black Jack, floors above them, thought of his driver, Fetch. "I tend to like westerns."

Krif Tayfyet scoffed. "The ones filled with men with pistols who waste as much brimstone as a merchant prince? Shooting at one another and missing?"

"What you're doing is different how?"

Krif Tayfyet said nothing and turned off his compass for a moment. Krif Lūwof was approaching.

"Achtāshhit at. Syārpip," the redcrown said.

"Syārpip? Mātsyār?" Krif Tayfyet asked.

"Krif Ruftu. Krif Lūho."

"Krif Luho? Both dead?"

The nod that came from Krif Lūwof's redcrown veiled his bitter face in a curtain of red flame.

Tayfyet frowned. "But Luho had the other hydrazite. And... *the faeflame.*" His face contorted. "We have to find him and kill him—*now.*"

The voice of the man who had now killed a handful of his best men came from the compass. "Laughy Taffy, you there?"

Tayfyet, concerned, angry, ashamed he'd been outwitted, said nothing.

40

YOUR SWORD AND SHIELD

"You said something about westerns," Ser Forty said. "Can you at least give me a western name to call you?"

"Wyatt."

"All right, Wyatt. All right."

"You the guy with two horses? They shot at?"

"You saw that?"

The man on the compass went quiet for a time. "Yeah," he said. "Yeah, that was bad. I'm glad you made it out okay."

"Me and my horse."

"What about the other one?"

"Didn't make it," Ser Forty said. "Are you doing okay, good Ser Wyatt?" He scratched his fat belly.

Captain Tsæt, who was watching while munching some meatball on a skewer, scoffed at Forty's lack of discipline.

Ser Forty stuck up his fat nose in response.

The man said, "Klūhman accents for many, but these guys come from all over. One's a redcrown and I've seen other things that make me think a good chunk are off-world."

"Half of Gergia's off-world. It's the off-world *world*."

The man scoffed. "Still. I have a feeling."

"Based on?" Ser Forty asked, swiping the skewer from his captain, who looked about ready to fire him.

"Well, they're loaded up with a dozen bullion of brimstone—*each*."

"Did you say a dozen bullion? I misheard."

"Each," the man confirmed.

"That's impossible," Ser Forty said. "People don't just carry around the operating budget of Megameso."

"These do," the man said. "And they *use* it. You saw the lightning."

"Brimstone weavers? I thought they died out."

Jack laughed, thinking of himself. What the world didn't know let it carry on in bliss. "Other heavy firepower I haven't quite figured out yet. They aren't playing footsie with politics or kidnapping."

Ser Forty peeked over the edge again, scanning level of windows after level of windows, hoping to catch a glimpse of a man, their lone wolf hero, gazing back. "How many?"

"Easily three dozen. Took out the charcoal corpse you saw."

"That was you? You killed a horse!"

"His fall did," Black Jack said. "I just tried to keep—"

"From killing me."

"Another down a shaft, buddy of the charcoal, and who knows how many with another thing."

"You're a weaver?"

"Don't talk about methods, it's a party line. But I've gotten creative. Seven downstairs, several dozen upstairs, and others between. I think three dozen's a solid guess, but whittling them. Whittling them."

"Well, keep it up," Ser Forty said.

Captain Tsæt had had enough of this jibber-jabber. He snatched the compass out of Ser Forty's hand.

"This is Captain Tsætŧeœuoˀꙡ, chief over the siege of this building," he said. "Who's this?"

"Wyatt, now, I guess. All right, okay. Put the knight on."

"I'm a knight myself and a commander of knights."

"Then put him on."

"Listen here." Captain Tsæt muffled the end and whispered to Ser Forty, "How do you know it's not *this* guy doing all this?"

Ser Forty opened his mouth to speak, but the man on the compass spoke first.

"Tsætŧeœuoˀꙡ?"

The captain looked shocked that someone had pronounced it right. "You gotta stop killing people willynilly. What do you want, man?"

"You think I'm the bad guy, Tsætŧeœuoˀꙡ? *I'm* the reason you even know the Common Realm was invaded. *Now put the other body on or I'll tell your dark secrets!*"

Tsæt threw the compass at Ser Forty. "Your witness," he said. "But if you find out before me that this guy's behind this whole thing and don't turn him in that second, I'll take your sword and shield."

"Only use the one anyways," Ser Forty said.

Tsætŧeœuoˀꙡ spat.

41

A PLUS ONE

Frey moved from the crowd of trembling guests dressed to the hilt toward Krif Tayfyet. Up the well-rounded low steps, a series of great concentric circles cut in half, stacked.

Into her office. Which Kif Tayfyet had made his headquarters.

"Well hello, flower pup," Krif Tayfyet said. "Have you come to keep me and the boys company?" He pulled up a chair and motioned to a lackey to pour some brandy.

"I've come to tell you that people need the latrine."

"Oh?"

She gestured behind herself to the crowd.

He followed her gesture. Saw he had a crowd on his hands who hadn't relieved themselves in quite some time—after dinner. How had he, a Klūhman, not prepared corrected action for such a root cause?

"Ah," he said. "Yes, then, in shifts. What else?"

"You have a very, very old man whose heart doesn't pump blood down to his feet properly, so surgeons rewired his heart as a kid to pump up to his head and let gravity do the work. In a building like this—"

"Fine, fine, fine," Krif Tayfyet said. "A delivery couch, Miz...?"

Frey glanced at the painting she'd hid behind the cabinet. Then she glanced at the drawer where she'd hidden Jack's love letters. "Sfansòrsiʔ," she said. "Frey Sfansòrsiʔ."

She thought of her daughter still hidden among the crowd.

Krif Tayfyet glanced around, trying in vain to follow her gaze, then asked, "You work here or a plus one?"

"Work."

"Anyone attend you?"

"You'd have to ask my assistant that question. I don't keep track of our 'honored guests,' " she said, using air quotes.

"Boyfriend? Husband?"

She hesitated. "Married to my work."

"Lose anyone?"

She didn't answer.

He looked around the office again, trying to find where her eyes had moved before. "Shame what happened to Hēme."

Pallor. On her face. "What happened to my boss?"

"Oh, you didn't know? We electrocuted him. And the seventeen."

Frey gasped.

"That's what happens to uncooperative Hollow Needle staff. Are *you* uncooperative?" He fiddled with a small platinum spearhead. A stylet, Frey knew.

She shook her head.

"Good. To the shitter, then, ten at a time."

42

DIGGING TILL NEXT YEAR

Fetch, the driver, finally looked up from his book and noticed his environment had subtly shifted over the hours. What had been a couple of drivers and valet boys grumbling among themselves had grown to a large crowd. Everyone but the more extreme introverts such as himself had exited their vehicles and had gathered a council in the middle of the lockdown stables.

"Building's under siege."

"Heard we can't get out any which way."

"One guy's digging. It'll take him longer than it will for the cavalry to arrive. He'll be digging till next year."

"Surety. Surety."

Fetch propped his book up, but he wasn't reading anymore.

Now he was listening. Understanding.

Learning what might come next.

43

BEAR CLAW

Ser Forty had been told to stay away from the building, but Captain Tsæt insisted on sending in the knights who actually wielded their swords. So Ser Forty got on the horn.

"Listen, Wyatt, I'm losing control."

The renegade called back, "What do you mean?"

"They're sending in knights."

"*To the tap?!* Did you hear what I said about the assassins?"

"Yes," Ser Forty said.

"There's children in here, and woozy-ass paper-pushing men. They—"

"I can only warn so much, Wyatt. I don't command the field."

"Dumbass captain of yours?"

Captain Tsæt eyed Forty, grimacing.

"Don't answer that, Ser Forty. Listen: do what you can to keep them from coming, or a lot—I mean a lot—of good men are gonna die."

Captain Tsæt rolled his eyes and shoved his hand

forward. Great faery lamps turned on all around the hillside, beacons and lanterns of old to send a warning or keep the valley illuminated. Secret fire glowed a white-hot steady glow, yet cold—light from another universe's sun—and magnified through Fresnel lenses fashioned from Tetra sands. They lit up the dark parts of the building so the watchers could see through the windows and beyond.

Fire, fireworks, and lightning exploded.

"Get down!" Captain Tsæt screamed.

The lightning struck the faery lamps. Small explosions in a quick crescendo.

Darkness fell once more.

Captain Tsæt growled. "Send in the crack team."

"Ser," Ser Forty said. "I don't know that..."

The captain was eating a roll of flatbread filled with grilled meats. He got on his compass and said, "Send 'em."

Three men ran up to the door and pulled out a device—woven at Nowthan's castle school— that would burn through the door. Bright flame on the locks. They were halfway through the job when some of the invaders shot bolts through the glass.

Not to kill the men. But enough to wound them.

Captain Tsæt was unfazed. "Send in backup."

They sent in backup to extract the wounded soldiers.

The backup got shot too.

"Send in the ram."

"Captain "

"Send in the ram."

The ram was a siege weapon they used in assaults on castles during prolonged battles. A team of ten horses pulled this one, a great bear claw, which swung freely on a great series of chains manned by two dozen armed knights.

44

SPLINTER AND SPARK

Upstairs, the men got a call from Krif Tayfyet. "Bring out the big boy."

Those on the seventh floor with angle enough on the ram hurried that massive slab of brimstone into place. The summoner had molten tattoos on his body. He called up *the entire brimstone slab*. Mind you, the damage so far had come from small bullion; this slab was coffin-sized.

They shattered the glass first to make a hole in the exterior wall, then the summoner pulled up a warp of lightning before the open hole in the wall. It writhed and filled their view. The summoner's companion turned his eyes away, but the dark eyes of the molten berserker had either been blinded or grown accustomed to such acts. To this massive sheet, he struck a match and added a simple flame, then directed the terrible amalgamation up.

It soared.

Struck the ram.

And exploded as when lightning hits a forest a dozen times.

Fire and splinter and spark and ash.
Above them, they heard the men groaning.

45

PILLAR OF FIRE

"Once more," Jack heard Krif Tayfyet say over the compass.

"Knock it off!" Jack said.

"Once more," Krif Tayfyet said.

"Tayfyet, you got them away from the front of the building. Let them pull back, get their men out, and regroup."

"Hit them *once more*," Krif Tayfyet said.

"Dammit, Tayfyet!"

Jack looked out and saw his absolute worst fear. The berserker, hanging out the window this time, shouted, *"Cwicuseolbur!"*

Two gallons of quicksilver streaked out of the great vial.

The summoner pointed at the ram. Probably to a dead man.

"Sanguidame knecht."

Black Jack tried to shoot at the berserker, but his lightning couldn't reach straight as a mere bolt. He wasn't as good at aim as these men; he'd spent far more time mixing lightning into things rather than shooting the raw element.

Five liters of blood shot up and wound into a midair spool that coagulated to the berserker's stylet. He wove it into the quicksilver, then pointed the swelling vermillion mass at the ram. It unraveled into enough strands to hit every man within.

"NO!"

It was an aggressive exsanguination weave. It struck. And though Jack could not see the men in the ram, he could hear their screams as their collective blood volume aeresoled into a puff of red mist.

The mist precipitated and rained blood on the ram.

Jack screamed in fury. He ran back to the bag containing the hydrazite, the little monster made of writhing transparent gelatin. Emptied it into a trashcan. Looked for a match, thinking he could shoot it, then looked in the bag once more.

Vials of faeflame.

He released a wicked laugh. Then started surrounding the hydrazite with the vials. He probably needed only one, but he added many, welded the trash can shut with spot weaving, and forced open the door of the descender.

He threw his makeshift explosive into the shaft.

It fell up.

And up.

Into the blackness until he couldn't see it anymore.

A little spark.

High above.

And then a great pillar of fire like the ignition of the rockets he'd heard about off-world.

He ducked and dove as it exploded outward.

Up above, the glass of the first ten floors and all the furniture exploded directly out of the walls. Along with a few dead bad guys.

Jack grinned to himself. Grinned. And then thought of Frey and Dövë.

He hoped his skills, at long last, were helping *them.*

46

BEG OFF

"Enough dickering about," said Sfòne. He rose from the tables near Dövë, who in her terror had taken to covering the white tablecloth with pastels, creating a portrait of the Archpivotal of Mogador, an old man with a full woven whip beard and bright orange beads all down the braids. In the picture, the man wore a ridiculous blue blazer cut into something like a frozen splash of water, along with a quilted long skirt made of the hats of many nations. The background showed his surrounding territories.

Sfòne could no longer wait around. He went straight for Frey's office, passing Frey on the way. She cocked her head but said nothing.

Sfòne stepped into her office, where the man in black and one of his henchmen were gathered.

"My gentlemen," he said, "it seems you're looking for that man who is causing so much trouble down below."

The room grew silent. Krif Tayfyet rose. "Who are you?"

Sfòne saw him glance at his blackpalm. "A friend of the man who's doing this to you, dear sirs. I suppose, from my experience, that I would call this situation just one more diplomatic negotiation, correct?"

Krif Tayfyet smiled.

"I can bring in your man," said Sfòne. "In exchange for your agreement not to hurt anyone."

"I agree," Krif Tayfyet said and grinned a full-toothed grin. He tossed his own onyx compass over to his unexpected visitor.

"Jack?" Sfóne said into the device. "Come in, dear Jack."

The line was silent.

"Jack?"

"Sfòne? What are you doing? Did you escape?"

"No, no, just trying to negotiate what's best with..." He looked up at the man in black.

"Krif Tayfyet," the Klūhman said.

"With Krif Tayfyet, Jack."

"Pit and Mirror, don't listen to Sfòne, Krif Tayfyet! I just met this guy tonight at the banquet."

"So you were at the banquet," Krif Tayfyet said. He whispered to Krif Lūwof, *Check the manifest.*"

Krif Lūwof departed.

"Whatever do you mean?" Sfòne asked. "We're old colleagues, Jack, dear old bosom boys."

Jack sounded desperate. "Tayfyet, this guy has no clue about any of this. He's a child. An addict."

Krif Tayfyet said, "Sfòne, ask him for my faeflame."

"Jack, give him the faeflame and we're going to get out of this."

"No, Sfòne, I will not do that. He has some sort of explosive somewhere in this building."

"Give it to him. He's given my word as a gentleman not to harm us." Sfòne nodded at Tayfyet.

Who nodded back, grinning still. Eager.

"Even if I got it to you, Sfòne, he'd kill you anyways. Leave the man alone. Beg off."

"An ambassador doesn't beg, Jack."

"You're no ambassador."

Krif Tayfyet yawned and killed Sfòne with lightning.

The thunder hurt Jack's ears on the other end. "For the love of the Author!" he shouted.

"Ah, you heard him die. Good," the Klūhman bandit said. "Perhaps you did not care about him, but we can keep going one by one if you wish. Now bring me my faeflame, or you will sorely regret it."

47

SIR FOUR T.

Captain Tsæt got on the radio. "Enough of you, Jack or Wyatt or whoever you are. I've got wood splinters and glass shards all over my—"

"What the hell?" Jack snapped. "Put the real knight back on. You're useless."

"You're the one who's useless," Captain Tsæt said. "You've destroyed ten floors of property."

"Trying to keep them from exsanguinating a couple dozen knights! *Now put the other man on!*"

Captain Tsæt threw the compass to Ser Forty. "Your witness," he muttered, and stormed off.

Ser Forty chuckled. "Hey there, Wyatt."

"Just call me Jack, they know that much now."

"Okay, Jack."

"What's your name?" Jack asked.

"Terence Thomas Tryban-Trevor."

"Good Author, your parents were cruel."

Terence chuckled. "Fast-food folks call me Ser Terence. Most of the guys call me Ser Forty."

"Like Four-T?"

"And forty."

Jack laughed.

"You on duty?" Forty asked. "You an agent of the state?"

Jack was silent. "I don't want to give much more about me just in case they can use it. Party line."

"Well, keep at it," said Forty. "I know the captain's an asshole, but he's under a ton of pressure, and a lot of my brothers in arms—they're so, so grateful to have someone like you on the front lines. Dunno how you're doing half the stuff you're doing, but we saw you try to shoot that one while he was throwing that blood thing."

"Trying ain't good enough."

"Well, keep at it anyways. You give us the faintest glimmer of hope for a way out of this long, dark hellhole."

48

TRIMBO

Krif Tayfyet hopped on the regional compass line. "Enough chatter," he said. "We demand at once the release of the following political hostages. The four Reygloans in the top of Ingenutvag Tower falsely accused of rerouting the Chickoa. The three dozen held in the Blazing World under accusation of assisting the Angler King in an insurrection. Jean Houdin from the pits of No'ad. Grim or other associates of the Faceless, currently housed in Guantanamo. All nine members of the Deviators, stored in the core vaults of Mars. The scattered lost legion of Trimbo."

Krif Lūwof mouthed, *Trimbo?*

Krif Tayfyet whispered, turning off the compass, "Heard about it in a bar downtown."

Into the compass he continued: "The five who staged a robbery in the skylights of Da'ad. And the South Transept twins. All released within the hour or we will execute one hostage every minute. We require transportation: a flying drake on the observation deck."

49

LAVA PLUMES

That was when the Inquisitors came. They had access to not just any aerial transportation, but a firefly, a great napalm-shooting insect.

Tayfyet *needed* that faeflame.

He went in search of it, down the descenders to the floor that contained the building's fashirals—and where his men had hidden their massive hydrazite monster beneath the catwalk. He tried to squeeze through a small opening between two tanks and the wall, but his brimstone and spear bulge caught. He had to empty his pockets and set his platinum spearhead stylet down on the railing behind the little gap before he could squeeze through. Then he climbed up to see if the faeflame had been hidden, and from that vantage he could also check on the base of the hydrazite, which had mostly stayed put, content to feast on small tanks of hydrogen and nitrogen.

"Easy now," said a voice below him. "Come on down."

Tayfyet froze. Could it be?

He edged down.

A man who could only be Wyatt—now Jack—stood before him in tight-fitting clothes, loose-fitting shoes that didn't match, and lava gloves. Lava gloves? Didn't those attract lava? Why was he wearing those? The man had a Crowfoot stylet pointing directly at Tayfyet, and he held a backpack that looked like it contained enough brimstone to cause some damage, along with a loose satchel.

Tayfyet dropped his Klūhman accent in favor of something more earthbound. "Mister, mister, mister, help," he said. "Evil men have taken the tower. The tower."

"The tap," Jack said.

"The tap! They've taken the tap tower," Tayfyet said, "and have killed so many. How do I get out of here?" He started back toward the spot where he'd left his spearhead stylet and brimstone.

"Whoa there, whoa there. Where you going? Did I tell you to go somewhere?"

Tayfyet's shoulders slumped, and he slunk back.

"Hop down," said Jack. "Let me look at you."

Tayfyet faced his foe.

Jack smiled. "There's bad guys all over this place. I'm gonna need your help. Do you know some basic weaves?"

Tayfyet nodded and kept up the frightened bystander act. "We... we... we had a teacher come through not long ago."

"Good. Take this." Jack passed him a stylet, probably taken from one of Tayfyet's own men, along with a small yellow rock he pulled from underneath his hat.

Tayfyet could hardly believe it—his foe was actually giving him weapons. Weapons Tayfyet would use to kill him.

Jack turned away from Tayfyet and said, "Let's go."

Tayfyet didn't follow. He pulled out his compass and, dropping the act and speaking in perfect Klūhman, summoned his men to his location.

Jack turned back—only to find Tayfyet pointing the stylet directly at him.

"Give me my faeflame," Tayfyet demanded.

"Nice to finally meet you, Tayfyet."

Tayfyet tried to call up the brimstone. It didn't work.

He tried again.

Again it failed.

"*Brynstane!*" he shouted.

Nothing happened.

This wasn't brimstone at all. Just a dumb yellow rock.

"You thought I'd just give you over raw brimstone, Tayfyet?" said Jack. He snatched the rock from Tayfyet's hands. "Let's go."

Just then, Tayfyet's men appeared, firing lightning.

Jack dodged and ducked out of the hall.

Krif Tayfyet squeezed back through the gap in the wall, retrieved his stylet and the brimstone brick, then jogged with it around the fashirals. His men were shooting left and right, but Jack somehow escaped into an area of desks and temporary walls and great open windowpanes that covered half of the level.

Tayfyet turned to the four men—including Krif Lūwof —who had come to save him. "He hides in this room, you dogs... and he wears lava gloves." He pointed out the window, where great lava plumes continued to spurt up beyond the gravity reversal shield.

His men understood, and together they called to the lava until it started shooting into the room. It blasted through the windows on every side and crept along the ceiling in a sheet, slowly turning the metal ceiling to slag as it ate everything it touched. But it seemed to be attracted to a far corner of the room near the stairs. There it pooled and descended from the ceiling.

Tayfyet smiled.

That was where Jack hid.

50

FOUNTAIN STOPPED FLOWING

lack Jack cried out in terror as the column of molten metal fell toward him. Jack knew jack about weaving lava. When it descended toward his hands and attached to the fingertips of the gloves, he stood and started running for the door. Still it climbed the fingers of the gloves, the end of a long strand that connected to the flow on the ceiling. As Jack ran he held his hands above him, little pillars of lava licking down his forearms as he went, creeping toward his exposed shoulders.

With the redcrown shooting blast after blast after him, Jack used one glove to pull off the other, used the bared hand to throw off the first, and then shouldered into the door of the stairwell, slamming it shut behind him.

Which mattered little, as it was reduced to so much slag.

He screamed in pain. The gloves had covered his hands and forearms, but extended only to his elbows. They had managed to keep the lava from actually touching bare skin, but the heat steaming off of them had burned his biceps black.

He'd dropped the satchel with the faeflame vials as he fled. He didn't care. He could focus only on the pain. He forced himself up the stairs several floors and staggered into a bathroom where he drew water into large sinks and submerged his burns.

Old blacksmith's trick: get the air away from the burn, not just the heat.

"Jack, you there?" Ser Forty said over the compass.

"Bits of me," Jack said.

Soaking, he looked out of the bathroom and saw an expensive fountain stocked with koi. He moved to the fountain and forced himself to submerge entirely into the cool water, gasping. Shock taunted him, and the koi pecked at his wounds. He used ambience, summoned Personification into the water, and had the water hand him a fish. He used the bone knife edge of his Crowfoot to skin it. Covered his wounds in fishskin. Scales and fishflesh would wetmeld to his skin and flake off, leaving a scarless bicep. He summoned another fish. And a third. And a fourth. Tossed the scraps.

Ser Forty spoke again. "Lava flooded a lower room. You weren't down there, were you?"

"Not anymore."

"You made it out?"

"Thanks to the early warning system."

"What's that?"

"A father angry with me for killing his son."

"Man."

"Why don't you swing a sword no more?"

Ser Forty sighed. "I don't want to talk."

"Even to a dying man as his last wish?"

"Low."

"Tending burns. Occupy my time."

"Battle of the Five Lakes."

"You were there?" Black Jack asked.

"I was in the middle where the paths meet, worst fighting. We had taken the field and pushed north to Florris to cast out our opponents. A young girl had picked up her father's sword. Screamed at me with it overhead. A haymaker. You know how those cheap towny swords are."

"Oh no."

"Yeah. I blocked it with mine. Her sword snapped in half, and she'd come at me so fast, part of her shard hit her in the chest and she ran clean into my blade. They found me holding her, refusing to pull it out."

Jack sat in silence.

The fountain suddenly stopped flowing.

"What's happening?" Jack asked.

"Inquisitors shut off the water. This is out of our hands now."

51

CORALITY & LIQUID SCILIAN

Krif Tayfyet looked to the man trying to crack the vault. "You asked about the water barrier?"

"I did," Tisyil said.

"And I told you the Inquisitors would come."

"They did."

"And what did they do?"

"Turned off the water."

The strongroom hissed and opened, and the men started dancing around joyfully as they looked at the millions of little boxes that contained full force info orders for the Archive.

"Seventy-seven million info orders for the ARC, the true currency of The Vale," Krif Tayfyet said. "Tisyil? What's the exchange?"

The scrawny man came forward and turned a page in his little notepad. "A quadrillion dollars for earthbound, fourteen thousand cubic tons of corality, a ton of liquid Scilian. Those are the core controvertible currencies."

Krif Tayfyet grinned. "Load them up. Quickly."

52

FIREFLY

As Tsæt and the Inquisitors listened, Krif Tayfyet's voice came over the compass. "I will take the prisoners to the basement observatory of the tap. Meet me with your transportation drake."

"As you wish," the Inquisitor replied, then muffled the compass.

"What now?" Captain Tsæt asked him.

The lead Inquisitor smiled. "Now we bring in the firefly instead of the drake they asked for."

53
STRONGBOXES

"But won't they be there?" asked Tisyil.

"What do you think that other long carriage was for?" Krif Tayfyet replied. "They'll be noodling with hostages in the basement while we're fleeing through the stables. We'll take the mountain threshold off-world and be in another mountain fort I've prepared, filling our info orders and monopolizing the data transfer to the archive."

Tisyil smiled as they loaded the orders into strongboxes with metal handles.

54

OFF THE COMPASS

lack Jack massaged the wet fishflesh so it stuck to his skin. Winced. Into the compass he said, "Forty, I need you to tell my wife something. She's never heard me ask her, *What do you need?* Let her know I was trying to meet her needs, okay? Let her—"

"Knock that off," Ser Forty said.

Black Jack paused as a thought struck him. "Tayfyet," he said to himself, "why were you down in the observatory by all those fashirals?"

He spoke once more into the compass. "Stay off the compass for a while, Forty, I'll be back."

"Hey, you're not getting down?"

"No, not like that. I... I think I might have stumbled on something we desperately need to know."

55

KEELT

Black Jack returned to the fashirals and went right back to that gap where Tayfyet had been. He looked everywhere around those little tanks and couldn't see much of anything. Then he looked down... and the light caught something shiny and gelatinous below the catwalk.

Jack took the metal grated catwalk down and came face to face with a hydrazite a hundredfold—no, a *thousandfold* —larger than the one he'd used.

Filled with faeflame vials, this one would blow the observatory clean off the bottom of the tap.

"Forty! Forty! Forty! Tayfyet lied. The observatory—"

He felt the point of steel.

Gingerly, he turned to find the redcrown Krif Lūwof pointing his sword-stylet at his cheek so that it drew a bit of blood.

"You killed my son," Lūwof said with a Klūhman accent so thick that *killed* sounded like *keelt*.

Sparks flew.

56

WHERE THEY'D KILLED THE 17

Tayfyet was bored with waiting, and returned to the ballroom floor. He searched through the desks to see what he'd find. Perhaps a nice letter opener he could sharpen and add to his weapon belt. Instead he found letter after letter that "Black Jack Dawes" had written to Ms. Frey. He also found her wedding band.

His eyes went wide at that, and he took in the office in a new light. From that wide-eyed perspective, he saw the blank, clean space on the wall where the painting had been —and then, searching, he found the missing painting tucked away behind a bookshelf.

He pulled it out to reveal his enemy, Jack, standing with Frey and a girl.

Dövë.

Everything clicked into place.

Tayfyet went out into the hall and shot a massive rippling bolt of lightning into the ceiling for good measure. It left a series of carbon scores as if the shadow of a great burning bush had laid on it.

"*Frey!*" he shouted. "Bring your daughter to me NOW."

Frey screamed.

So did Dövë.

But with all of the ambassadors and serving people huddling like mice, who could save them?

He shoved Frey—*Mrs. Dawes*—and her daughter into the descender and instructed it to take them to the strongroom floor. The very floor where they'd killed the seventeen ambassadors.

Meanwhile the rest of Tayfyet's men were ushering everyone else into the stairwell, forcing them down, down, down to the observatory.

57

30%

The Inquisitors were flying the firefly fast toward the observatory. Captain Tsæt was riding along.

"Isn't this rather dangerous for the innocents?" he asked.

"Very," one of the Inquisitors said. "Nearly thirty percent will lose their lives in this maneuver."

"*Thirty percent?!* That's a third of the world's diplomats!"

"It's the easiest way to save the rest," the Inquisitor said.

Ser Forty came on the compass. "Pull it back," he said. "Tayfyet's lying."

"About what?" Tsæt asked.

"Unsure, but it has to do with the observatory."

The Inquisitors scoffed and said, "Turn it off."

They flew down the great, wide crater even faster.

58

COME DIE

The redcrown Krif Lūwof was electrocuting Jack, but slowly. The pain went through Jack's mind like a pulsing of every fire that had ever scalded him, but on the inside, every bone a funny bone, and every funny bone shattering.

And yet, through it all, Jack laughed.

Lūwof paused and leaned close to his prisoner. "What's so funny?"

Jack grabbed the handle of the stylet, twisted, yanked it free, and threw it across the floor through the open shaft doors.

The two men matched each other blow for blow. Boxes. Parries. Chokeholds. A leg sweep from Jack. But Jack was getting the living hell kicked out of him. The redcrown was bigger, faster, better in every way, and Jack was still weakened from the electrocution, not to mention the lava burns.

Eventually the redcrown stood tall before the shaft, framed like a dark angel in an eldritch light, poised like a prizefighter, and said, "Come, Jackie. Come die."

Jack swished blood in his mouth and spat it at the man's eyes.

Lūwof covered them.

And Jack reared back with all his remaining strength and kicked Krif Lūwof into the shaft.

He heard him bounce a few times on the way up, but instead of waiting to hear him hit the first floor above, he summoned one of the other descenders to take it one floor up, snatching the man's leftover brimstone as he did.

59

GOING FAST

J ack dispatched the three guards in the observatory. Through one dead guard's compass, he heard Frey's screams and Tayfyet saying, "Once you're done down there, meet us in the strongroom."

Jack had no time for this. No time. He was a bloody mess in a too-tight tunic, too-loose pants, sloppy shoes that didn't match, blood and scars and burns and black soot, half a head of hair singed off.

He shouted at the crowd of people who had been herded here. *"Get back downstairs! Or, upstairs! Whatever way is out in this damn tap, just go back the way you came!"*

They simply stared at him in horror and confusion.

So he used a good chunk of the redcrown's brimstone to call up a storm.

That got them moving for the stairwells...

... just as the Inquisitors showed up on a firefly the size of a war galley.

"That's one of the bad guys," said the lead Inquisitor. "Look at him terrorizing the people."

Jack shouted at them. *"Same army!"*

The firefly shot pillars of fire out its ass and mouth, blowing holes in the glass. The people had escaped the level and sprinted up the stairs, but Jack hadn't.

And this platform wasn't going to hold.

So he dropped his drawers.

He *hated* when he had to do this. But he'd been told that, in a pinch, when nerves were on, pissweaving was the best skill he could know. So he'd learned it first, even as the other weavers in training mocked him. And he'd be damned if pissweaving hadn't saved him early and often.

He peed all over the floor, with glass furniture serving as a shield and buffer. Then he called up the piss into a warp and called up the remaining ghosts of the stone in the sand that had melted into the glass shards all around him.

A great coiled rope rose up like a frozen stream from a fountain.

A yellow one.

He quickly tied it off to the steel emergency stairwell.

Then he looked through the broken glass wall, up and out into the crater, and hated himself.

That table?

The one he'd charred and crushed Forty's stray horse with?

He was about to repeat its journey.

And he hated—*hated*—going fast.

But Black Jack jumped anyway.

Over the compass he heard Tayfyet scream, "BLOW IT NOW!"

Behind him, every pane of glass shattered and the Inquisitors and the captain and the firefly were all blown down into the lava.

But Jack?

Jack was falling *up* with naught but a piss-rope to hold

him. He shot up the full length of the tap, passing the fiftieth floor, then the forty-second with the ball. That was when he reached the end of his rope.

And it snapped.

Jack kept going.

He was free-falling, full speed up toward the tenth floor. Then the platform. Then beyond.

The force of reversed gravity threw him up into the air over the crowd of knights and Inquisitors surrounding the entrances to the lobby. Past the gravitational field in a massive arc over the entrance.

Gravity reasserted itself, and his fall up turned into a fall down.

A hundred knights and soldiers watched him fly. They were silent and awkward. He was screaming like an infant child.

He passed the platform and bridges clean to the other side of the tap and plummeted through normal gravity into the hole on the other side.

Reverse gravity reasserted itself, and he slowed, pulled toward the building. He called up some wind—he wasn't a skyweaver, but he could give himself a nudge—and he caught the edge of the shattered ninth-floor and pulled himself in before he had to do the whole thing over again.

He promptly puked.

Then looked outside.

Then puked outside while looking.

The volcano wasn't erupting, but the lava had crept up outside the reverse gravity shield to cover the stone wall and leave nothing but a ring of fire around the tap.

60

WHEELS CAME OFF THE WAGON

Down in the stables, Fetch saw the man who'd cracked the water barrier getting a stable boy ready to drive away the largest carriage there. He watched as the man pulled off a sheet of fabric to reveal a very large medic and barber surgeon carriage. Something about the carriage, and the man's behavior, made Fetch suspicious.

So he went over there and took the pins out of the carriage wheels, one by one.

Then he shouted at the stableboy, saying, "He's one of them! One of the reasons we're stuck here! Stop the dog!"

The stableboys and drivers, bored out of their gourds, wanted any reason to use all that pent-up energy. They surrounded the medic carriage, and the safecracker tried to whip the horses and flee.

The wheels came off the wagon.

And the stableboys descended on him.

61

GRAVITIES NEGATED

J ack had no brimstone, but he still had his stylet. He went to the lift and took it straight to the strongroom floor.

Stylets can be fashioned from anything, as long as they're long, slender, and made from something unique to the storyweave. Show-offs picked swords and spears, sometimes marble pillars. Black Jack's Crowfoot blended into his cap's black band—like a tiny feather, the tiny bone. With no brimstone, stylet hid, he walked into the strongroom, screaming, *"Tayfyet, you mutt!"*

Tayfyet stilled and spat, pointing his stylet at Frey and Dövë. He was flanked by two of his men, each of them wearing three large bags of brimstone, both pointing stylets at Black Jack.

"Well," said Tayfyet. "It seems you've lost, Jacksie."

Dövë recalled at that very moment how Sfòne had described, in detail, his mother, Tayfyet's sister, who had died under mysterious circumstances. By Dövë's best guess, Tayfyet had killed his sister, Sfòne's mother. She started pulling on all of the descriptions of Sfòne's mother and directed those thoughts toward the chalked stone crumbles on the floor halfway between Tayfyet and Frey and herself and Jack.

The chalk floated up.

Tayfyet gasped.

Dövë directed the chalk with her mind so that it spelled out words on the wall:

TAYFYET. THIS IS AYMU, YOUR SISTER. YOU HAVE BEHAVED ABYSMALLY.

Tayfyet startled, wide-eyed. "No, no. This—"

Meanwhile Jack focused his will on the three bags, plucked his Crowfoot from his hat, and called up the brimstone from everywhere at once.

Weaving is first and foremost about using one's will on the raw elements of the narrative world and submitting them to logoi: the logics of various things. It has a little bit to do with willpower, but it's mostly about yielding mind to Mind and paying attention to the natures of things. Try as the others might to recall their own brimstone, Jack had the upper hand—and a whole lot of lightning. He called up stone and wove it into three long spears of firelight.

The spears shot straight through two of the men, killing them instantly, but merely pierced through Tayfyet's shoulder. He didn't die, but was sent careening toward the shattered window behind him, towing Frey by the antigravity bracer Sfòne had given her. Tayfyet stumbled right out the window and immediately fell up in the reverse gravity, hanging on only by Frey's bracer.

Jack ran forward and struggled to free Tayfyet from the bracer.

As Tayfyet pulled his spearhead stylet to stab Jack's wife.

The bracer came loose first—and what happened next shocked all three of them.

Tayfyet didn't fall.

He didn't fly.

He floated in place, both gravities negated.

So Jack reared back and kicked him toward the orange glow.

Krif Tayfyet tried to swim the opposite way, but he floated backward through the gravitational barrier and hit the ring of fire and lava.

There he was no more.

Dövë buried her face in her papa's chest.

62

COLD

Downstairs, the three of them met Ser Forty, who said, "I told you you'd see her again, didn't I?"

"You did," Black Jack said to the fat man.

"I told—"

A scream. The redcrown emerged from the lobby with his sword and swung it at Jack, his full weight behind the blow.

Jack was caught unawares and completely defenseless against the blow.

But it didn't strike him.

Ser Forty had drawn his own sword and blocked the redcrown's.

The redcrown's sword snapped in half, just as the little girl's had so long ago, and his own momentum ended up killing him when his body met Ser Forty's blade.

After the mess, Jack asked, "What's that thing made out of?"

"Sicilian," said Forty.

Fetch chose that moment to pull up in his chariot. One of the spokes had a bit of charring and one of the lamps had shattered, but compared to the busted down transportation around them, it seemed the finest ride for miles around. "Where to?"

"Somewhere cold," Jack said.

Frey looked at her husband's wounds. "Preferably with running water."

AFTERWORD

Thanks for reading Tap and Die. I hope you enjoyed the journey. I highly encourage you to check out other stories in the Vale universe, starting with the **Vale Short Stories series**, each of which also comes in audiobook format. Also connected to this story in lesser or greater detail:

- **Bell Hammers: The True Folk Tale of Little Egypt** — historical novel
- **The Greenwood Poet** — poetry
- **Harry Rides the Danger** — picture book
- **Cold Brewed** — photo novel
- **Of Gods and Globes I & II** — fantasy and sci fi stories
- **The Elevator Out** — picture book
- **Inconveniences Rightly Considered** — poetry

You can always check out lanceschaubert.org for resources on your own fiction, serialized stories, life updates, and to make sure you're on the inside when I release anything new.

We also published some 500 international authors, artists, and academics during the 3 years surrounding the pandemic, so there's a huge archive of works available for free on there. You can find my email on the site and drop me a line or join our Discord — we always enjoy hearing from you and respond as soon as we're able.

Unconditional love and respect and confidence until *The End*

— Lancelot

www.ingramcontent.com/pod-product-compliance
Lightning Source LLC
Chambersburg PA
CBHW030642190726

48286CB00008B/2616